The Fuhrer Document

The Fuhrer Document

A Story About the Fourth Reich

A novel by
Jerry R. Barksdale

iUniverse, Inc.
New York Lincoln Shanghai

The Fuhrer Document
A Story About the Fourth Reich

All Rights Reserved © 2004 by Jerry R. Barksdale

No part of this book may be reproduced or transmitted in any form or by any means, graphic, electronic, or mechanical, including photocopying, recording, taping, or by any information storage retrieval system, without the written permission of the publisher.

iUniverse, Inc.

For information address:
iUniverse, Inc.
2021 Pine Lake Road, Suite 100
Lincoln, NE 68512
www.iuniverse.com

This book is a work of fiction. Any resemblances to actual events, locales or persons, living or dead is entirely coincidental.

ISBN: 0-595-31370-1

Printed in the United States of America

To the men and women who fought the forces of darkness
during World War II and saved democracy.

This book would not have been possible without the expert advice and skillful hand of my editor, Karen Middleton of Athens, Alabama.

Chapter 1

▼

"Hitler's SS is up there. A mean bunch of bastards. Remember Malme'dy, where they cut down eighty-six with machine guns—after they had surrendered."

Second Lt. Kubinski, a New Yorker, paused and squinted up at the cloud-covered peak above the Bavarian village. "It's our job to take that piece of real estate."

The hard-bitten paratroopers stirred and looked at each other without comment. Sgt. Jabo Jackson slouched his six-foot, 200-pound frame against a stone building, chewing a twig, an M-1 at his side. He pushed back his steel pot revealing a shock of coarse black hair and looked up. Snow-covered peaks sparkled in the morning sun. He was a long way from North Alabama, where now his folks would be busy planting cotton and corn.

The young lieutenant continued, "Headquarters says there's some major krauts with SS tight as stink on shit. So watch your ass and don't take any unnecessary chances. I don't want to lose any men. One more thing. No looting! Understand?"

The soldiers listened silently.

Kubinski looked at Pfc. Hurston Snoddy, a lanky kid with a stutter from Pine Level, Alabama. "Remember, Snoddy, if you bag one more kraut, you're eligible for the supreme sacrifice."

Snoddy looked away and spat on the ground.

"Sergeant Jackson!" Kubinski barked.

Jabo looked at the lieutenant and removed the twig from his mouth without straightening.

"Yes, suh."

"Take a squad and move up along the road. I'll take the rest of the platoon and spread out through the woods. Any questions?"

"No, suh."

"Good luck, and be careful."

Jabo slung his M-1 over his shoulder, hitching a thumb in the sling. "All right men, you heard the lieutenant. Saddle up. Let's git this damn war over with so we can go home. Everybody keep thirty feet apart." The soldiers stirred and grumbled.

Jabo led his men single file down the cobblestone street, still slick from a shower, and across a bridge spanning a narrow river, then trudged up the steep road, zigzagging to the top of the peak. The only sounds were creaking leather and heavy breathing.

Near the plateau, Jabo stopped. He pushed back his helmet, mopped his brow, lit a Lucky and surveyed his front. The morning stillness was interrupted only by the chirp of birds. Good sign. Shards of sunlight pierced the treetops to a profusion of wild flowers poking up from the forest floor. Feeling more confident, he glanced behind him and beckoned Snoddy.

Snoddy slouched up to Jabo.

"Y-you hear what the sumbitch y-Yankee lieutenant said?"

"Yeah, I heard em," said Jabo.

"H-he's always on my case. Like h-he wants to get me killed."

"He's just having some fun with ya."

"Soon as this w-war's over, I'm headin to sweet h-home Alab-bama."

"Yeah. Now listen, when we reach the top up there, you stick with me."

"Y-you can count on me."

"What if we found Hitler's very own dagger and pistol, Snoddy? Reckon what it'd be worth back home?"

"Ain't no t-tell'n. Reckon ol Hitler's up there along with them other krauts like the lieutenant s-said?"

"Nah, I figure they've already hightailed it down to South America. But you know something, Snoddy?"

"W-what?"

"They couldn't carry all their loot with 'em so they've left some behind...for you and me."

A big grin spread across Snoddy's face.

Jabo eyed the smaller man. "Keep your mouth shut. Understand?"

Snoddy nodded. "S-sure. How 'bout a nail, Jabo?"

Jabo shook a cigarette from the pack and Snoddy fired it with a Zippo.

Jabo signaled for the squad to move forward, their rifles at port arms. On top, where the terrain leveled out, Jabo paused. Explosions had stripped trees bare and bomb craters pockmarked the earth. Buildings were blown apart, only a few stone walls standing amidst smoldering ruins. The British Air Force had done one hell of a job. Jabo paired his men in twos and fanned them out to search the damaged buildings.

"Snoddy, you stay with me."

"Y-yeah, Jabo."

The two moved cautiously toward a two-story blackened brick structure, Snoddy walking backward rifle at ready, covering their rear. They saw no movement when they cased the outside of the building.

"Let's take a look-see." Jabo pointed at the open door. He darted inside, his M-1 poised and ready and Snoddy close behind. The place was large and appeared to have been a police headquarters—maybe Gestapo. Jabo signaled to Snoddy to search upstairs. He soon returned, finding nothing. They split up, each taking a separate room.

"J-Jabo!"

Jabo bolted into the room where Snoddy stood in front of an open door. "Not so damn loud. What is it?"

"L-look!" Snoddy pointed.

Jabo peeked through the open door where a stairwell led down into a black hole. "Shhhh." He poked his head inside the stairwell, listening for several seconds, but heard nothing. Slinging his rifle, he pulled out a .45 and inserted a full clip of seven, then chambered a round and cocked the hammer. The pistol was his favorite weapon. Back home in Alabama, before the war, he had shot tin cans off fence posts with his dad's old .38.

"Cover me," he said.

They crept down the narrow, spiral staircase, Jabo raking the brick walls with the beam of his flashlight. The air became colder the deeper they descended. They reached the bottom fifty or more feet below, where a long, domed tunnel, nearly wide enough for a Jeep, angled off. The passage was dark and dank, smelling of mildew.

"S-shit, what is this?"

"A bunker, asshole."

Jabo eased forward, flashlight in one hand, .45 in the other. Snoddy covered their rear. Water dripped from the ceiling and splattered on the brick floor, echoing down the long passageway.

"This place gives me the w-willies."

"I see light. Watch our asses while I check it out." Jabo clicked off the flashlight and crept into the grayness. Light spilled from a half-open door and he stopped a few feet short and listened. Hearing nothing but the pounding of his heart, he eased closer. Hugging the cold tunnel wall, he slowly craned his head to peek between doorjamb and hinges. No one. Glancing back over his shoulder at Snoddy, Jabo slowly pushed open the door, then stepped inside the room, pistol clamped in both hands, sweeping from side to side. Empty. Jabo lowered the automatic. He looked around at what appeared to be a storage area. Several olive drab boxes with the eagle and swastika emblem of the Third Reich sat on the floor. Jabo walked to the door and motioned for Snoddy. Snoddy sprang inside the room, his eyes darting. "W-Whatcha got Jabo?"

"Watch the door while I check out these boxes."

Snoddy stepped to the opening, while Jabo holstered his Colt and pried open a wooden box.

"Well, what do ya know. Daggers! Pretty shiny ones with black handles." Jabo lifted one out and unsheathed it. "SS."

"L-let me see."

"You keep your eyes peeled. I'm going to check out these other boxes." Jabo pried open the top of a flat wooden container and removed the packing material on top. "You ain't gonna believe this, Snoddy. Lugers. A whole damn box full!"

"Aw, come on"

"I ain't shittin ya. Snoddy, we done hit the jackpot. There ain't a man in the outfit that wouldn't give a month's pay for one. Boy, we gonna be rich."

Snoddy left his post, making for the open box. "B-boy howdy. Ain't we s-stumbled on sumthin? This is gonna be easier than p-pickin apples."

Jabo grabbed two of the pistols and crammed them behind his webbed cartridge belt. Snoddy took three.

"We need something to tote 'em in," Jabo said. Let's check out the rest of this bunker."

Jabo unholstered his .45 and they made their way back into the murky tunnel.

After several yards, the tunnel abruptly made a ninety-degree turn to the left, where in front of them, a shaft of light pierced the darkness. Another side room, maybe. They crept nearer. Jabo, hearing something, signaled Snoddy to halt. At the far end of the tunnel metal clanged like a gate swinging open. They froze.

"Somebody's coming. Be ready."

A clicking rustle, many feet, coming fast. But not the heavy booted footfalls of men. Panting, whining. Dogs!

"Git down!" he rasped.

Both men dropped to the cold, wet floor. Against the faint light, three large dogs were charging fast. Jabo leveled the automatic and fired three times in quick succession. Sharp yelps, then two dogs stumbled, pitching forward jowls down onto the brick. Snoddy got off a shot, but missed. A black Doberman sprang at Snoddy knocking him backward, and went for his face. Snoddy dropped his rifle and grasping the snapping, snarling creature by the upper and lower jaws as they thrashed about on the wet floor.

"H-help me!"

Jabo stuck his pistol to the dog's head. Blood and brains sprayed the wall and the creature fell limp. Snoddy rolled it off him.

"That was c-close," he gasped. "Sumbitch almost t-tore my throat out."

"Let's go!" Jabo barked, grabbing Snoddy by the collar and jerking him to his feet.

A tall man in a black SS uniform stepped from a lighted doorway, aimed a pistol at Jabo, fired and missed. Jabo's Colt barked twice, one shot drilling the guard's forehead. He fell backward, his pistol clanging to the bricks. Jabo sprang through the open doorway. There was a movement. Another black-clad figure with a brown leather satchel and a pistol fired, but bolted as Jabo returned fired. Both men missed their marks, bullets pinging off stone walls. The guard dropped his pistol and reached for the ceiling.

"*Nein—nein!*"

"*Ich spreche kein Deutsch!*" Jabo yelled the only German words he knew. "Talk English, you son of a bitch!"

"Don't shoot!" cried the German.

Snoddy rushed up, pumping another round into the dead German, then sprang into the room. He pointed his M-1 at Jabo's captive.

"Leave 'em be Snoddy, he's give up. Get his sidearm and search 'im." Jabo ejected the ammo clip from the pistol, inserted a full one, and ratcheted a round into the chamber.

Snoddy picked up the P-38 the German had dropped then searched him.

"He's c-clean."

"Keep a look out," Jabo said, gesturing toward the doorway.

Snoddy stepped into the passageway and knelt over the dead guard, pried open his mouth and peered inside.

Jabo kept the .45 aimed at his prisoner's head. From the silver skull on his black visor cap and the two stripes on his collars, he knew him to be an SS lieutenant—*Oberstrumfuehrer*.

"Anyone else around?" Jabo asked, never taking his eyes off the man.

"*Nein.*"

"Dammit, I said talk English!"

"No one else is present."

"One move and you'll be in Valhalla with your buddy out there. Now set that satchel on the floor. Real slow."

The lieutenant, tall and broad-shouldered with blue eyes of ice and short blonde hair, slowly lowered the satchel to the floor.

Jabo moved around, keeping and eye on his captive, to see out the doorway at the same time. Snoddy was down over the dead German working inside his gaping mouth with a pair of pin-nosed pliers.

"Wha'cha doing Snoddy?"

"P-prospectin for gold. This sumbitch got better teeth 'n me!" He extracted a gold tooth.

"You crazy, ignorant low life. Get your ass in here!"

Snoddy deposited the gold tooth into a bulging tobacco sack and went for a gold band on the dead man's finger. He tried to work the ring off, but couldn't get it past the knuckle. He pulled out his bayonet and hacked off the finger, dropping the ring into his sack with the tooth.

"Keep an eye on him," Jabo said, eyeing Snoddy with disdain. "Shoot 'em if he blinks."

"M-my pleasure." Snoddy pulled the Mauser from his waist, chambered a cartridge and pointed.

Jabo's eyes swept the room. He noticed a thick steel door swung back against the wall. The room looked like a vault. He picked up the leather satchel near the German's feet, snapped it open and pulled out a sweater, pants, socks and shoes, flinging them on the floor.

"Looks like our friend was planning a vacation," Jabo said as he pawed through the satchel and lifted out a bundle of reichsmarks. "He's even got some traveling money."

"H-how much, Jabo?"

"A whole heap." It was more money than Jabo had ever seen in his life. He looked around the room. "We need something to put the money in. Go look down the hallway and find a sack or something. And be careful."

Snoddy bolted out the door. Jabo aimed his .45 at the German's head with one hand, cramming bundles of money inside his field jacket with the other.

Two rapid gunshots shattered the silence. Snoddy cursed and screamed. Jabo sprang to the doorway and saw the back of a black uniformed man running away. He fired once and his target pitched forward. Snoddy was on his back, not moving, blood spreading around him. Jabo swung the automatic around at his prisoner, whose hands were still high over his head.

"You lying Nazi bastard. I'm gonna kill you."

"I know where there are more reichsmarks," the lieutenant said.

"Talk fast."

Jabo's eyes caught movement in a pile of blankets in the darkened corner. He swung and fired.

"*Nein, nein*! No more shooting!"

A small child of five or six crawled from beneath the blankets, crying and trembling.

"Who's the kid?"

"*Mein* friend, if you let me and the child pass, I will make you rich."

"I'm not your damn friend," Jabo snarled.

"Very rich."

Jabo studied the man a moment, then the kid. A good-looking tyke with blonde hair was wearing short black pants, knee-high white socks and a wool sweater. His eyes brimmed with unshed tears.

Very rich. Sure beat hell out of chopping cotton. "Start talking."

"Permit us to pass and you can have the reichsmarks in the satchel and the others over there." He gestured with his head toward a box. "There's more, much more down the passageway."

Jabo moved over to the box, opened the lid and saw stacks of reichsmarks.

"Why don't I just shoot your ass and keep the money?"

"What about the child? Could you be so cruel?"

Jabo pondered for a moment. "Get your ass out of here before I change my mind."

The lieutenant reached to pick up the satchel.

"Leave that. Now git!"

"Let me take it out, and you take the reichsmarks."

Jabo waved his pistol at the German.

"Please."

"Git, I said!" He tightened his finger on the trigger.

The German grabbed the child by the hand and they fled down the passageway.

Jabo stuffed his pockets with money and documents—everything in the satchel—until they were bulging, then stuffed all he could into his bloused pant legs, then he went to check on Snoddy. Snoddy lay face up, white and waxy as a candle. Dark blood congealed around two holes above his left pocket. Jabo cursed. He shouldn't have sent Snoddy out alone. Too late now. He lifted out the tobacco sack, jerked the Mausers from Snoddy's belt and fled the bunker.

Chapter 2

▼

Hardy Jackson rolled over and squinted at the red numbers glowing on the nightstand. It was always the same. He awoke promptly at 4 a.m. and the same scenario played in his mind, as he reviewed every pending case in the office. Answers filed within the legal time limit? Subpoenas issued? Sometimes he'd even try a case in his head. Judge Fagan was always scowling down at him from the bench. At that point in his mental screenplay, he gave up on sleep and rolled out of bed.

He pushed back the covers slowly, careful not to wake Millie who was lying on her back and snoring softly, her pale hair splayed against the white pillow. A shaft of light from the street lamp sliced through a gap in the drapes, casting a dull beam across the king-size bed. He leaned close. Her full lips fluttered slightly each time she exhaled. She'd put on a few pounds, but she was just as desirable as the first time he'd seen her at an Auburn pep rally on Toomers Corner 21 years ago. She was a music major from Montgomery and he was in pre-law and playing tackle for the Tigers.

He pressed his lips to her forehead, then swung his bare feet onto the carpet and tiptoed out of the bedroom.

Downstairs, he measured out coffee and waited for the steaming black liquid to fill the pot. He savored the aroma while doing deep breathing and stretching exercises.

With a piping mug in one hand and a legal pad in the other, he went to the old blue plaid couch in the den, where he eased his big frame into one end. That's where he did his writing. It was a ritual. An hour and a half every morning, come what may. He sipped coffee and began a new scene for his thriller, a story about a small town Southern lawyer, who, while representing a client in a drug case, discovered that the local judge was the actual kingpin of the drug ring. The plot was goofy and writing not very good, but he kept at it anyway, seven days a week.

Aubie, a gray tabby Millie had found half starved and yowling at the back door several years earlier, jumped on the couch and curled up. Hardy stroked the cat's head, then glanced up at the mantel clock. He was running late. He gathered the yellow pages filled with his longhand and counted them. Four. After editing, he guessed he'd end up with one good typed page. Not a lot, but a page a day equaled a novel in a year. When he sold his book, and after the publisher's check cleared the bank, he had a list of people as long as his leg he intended to call and tell them to kiss his honky white ass. Judge Betty Fagan's name was at the top. Bitch. He hated the Judge. He hated the law. He hated his clients.

Hardy stashed the manuscript in his briefcase, wolfed down a glazed donut Millie left for him on the kitchen counter, then tiptoed upstairs and dressed in camo.

*   *   *   *

Hardy swung the blue 1978 Jeep Wagoneer into his father's driveway and honked twice. The Jeep had over 200,000 miles on the odometer, but he babied it and changed the oil religiously every 3,000 miles. He turned around and clucked to the two dogs in the backseat and they yelped back eagerly. Moments later, the storm door at the side of his father's house flew open and Jabo emerged, pulling on his brown hunting cap, vapor clouds puffing from his nostrils. A .16 gauge Browning was cradled in the crook of his arm. He was a big-boned man with broad shoulders and brown eyes. Everyone said his son was his dead ringer.

Hardy reached across the seat and opened the passenger door and Jabo climbed in, grunting. He placed the shotgun on the backseat.

"Mornin' pop. How ya' feeling?"

"Tolerable, for an old fart," Jabo said. "How 'bout you?"

"Ready and rarin' to bag the limit."

Jabo twisted around and looked at the two dogs in the backseat. One was a young, liver-spotted pointer. The older dog was an English setter.

"I see you brought the whelp along," Jabo said. "Hell, all she'll do is scare up the birds."

Hardy didn't comment. There were three things that his father knew more about than any man in French Springs: quail hunting, used cars and good whiskey. Hardy and Jabo had hardly missed a Saturday quail hunting during the season, especially since Hardy's mother died three years earlier.

Hardy backed out of the driveway and headed down the street, past a row of modest brick ranchers. Jabo noted that smoke rose straight up from an occasional chimney. "No wind. That's good." he said. "The birds will be out feedin."

Hardy nodded.

"How's Millie 'n Clint?" Jabo asked. "Ain't seen 'em 'n forever."

"Clint's fine. He called last night. Said he's transferring to Alabama next fall. Can you believe it?"

"Well, shit fire!" Jabo looked dumbfounded. "What's wrong with that boy, anyhow?"

"I don't know. Beats me. As for Millie, she's still meaner'n hell." Jabo chuckled.

"That gal's a pistol. A man don't appreciate a good woman till she's gone. There ain't a day passes that I don't miss yer mama."

Hardy grew serious. "Truth is, I'm worried about her. Lately, she's been wheezing like a freight train and coughing her dang head off. Damn cigarettes. She smokes two packs of Marlboros a day."

Jabo frowned, tapped a Lucky from his pack, screwed it in the corner of his mouth and lit it.

"It wouldn't hurt you to quit, either," Hardy said, shooting a dark glance at his father.

"Aw hell, I got one foot 'n the grave and the other on gooseshit," Jabo said, pulling deeply on the Lucky.

"Don't talk like that, Pop."

"Son, I ain't what I once was. If the Lord would give me a contract for seventy-five, I'd sign it in a New York minute. But Millie's got a lot of living 'head of 'er. You get her to a doctor, you hear?"

"Yes, sir."

"How bout running by the car lot, son. I got a pint of Rebel Yell 'n the desk. It's mighty cold today and I might need a touch to warm up my insides."

Hardy circled the brick cobblestone town square. In the center, surrounded by rows of shabby brick buildings, sat a three-story red brick courthouse capped by a tarnished copper dome, built in 1905. He drove two blocks west on Lee Street and turned in under a large painted tin sign: "Jabo's Fine Used Cars." Below, in smaller letters was: "Go to church on Sunday, see Jabo on Monday."

Hardy waited in the Jeep while Jabo went inside the small mobile home that served as an office. It was the same house trailer the family had lived in until

Hardy was in the third grade, when they moved into the rancher on the edge of town.

In a few minutes, Jabo returned to the Jeep and uncapped the whiskey.

"Turn 'yer head son." He took a long pull on the sour mash and grimaced. "Wowee! This damn stuff hurts so good."

"Pop, that stuff's zapping your brain and petrifying your liver."

"Yeah, well."

Hardy drove past the large spring for which the town was named, now a duck pond surrounded by a public park, then stopped for a northbound freight. After the train passed, Hardy headed north toward Tennessee's rolling gray hills.

"Did you happen to see that program on A&E Tuesday night about World War II?" Hardy asked.

"Nah."

"It was good. Called 'The Final Days of World War II.' There was a segment about the Normandy Invasion and the Battle of Bastogne. I was just thinking, weren't you there?"

"Yeah." Jabo stared out the window and puffed his cigarette.

"You never told me about it," Hardy said. "I guess you know about the fiftieth anniversary ceremony the American Legion is sponsoring."

"I heard about it."

"Well, you should attend. It's to honor you and others who fought in the war."

His father took another pull on the Rebel Yell and wiped his mouth with the back of his hand. "I'd just as soon leave it back there. No sense diggin it all up again."

"Where do you think we'll find the birds this morning?"

"Let's try the 'ol Tuten Plantation in that sedge field on top of the ridge."

"That's a long walk. You sure you're up to it?"

"Yeah, I need to stretch my legs."

The Tuten Plantation was 2,000 acres of rolling hills and rich creek bottoms. Rundown and overgrown with brush, it had once been a showcase for splendid Tennessee walking horses and rich with tobacco and corn. Hardy pulled off the pavement and parked next to Taylor's cotton gin, which was closed for the season, and unloaded the dogs. In high school, he'd worked Saturdays at the gin until a workman got his hand caught in the razor sharp gin teeth. When they pulled him out, only a few scraps of flesh remained on the bones of his arm. Jabo made him quit.

Hardy and his father walked a mile or more down a field road along a fence row covered over with sumac and sassafras bushes. They came to the Tuten plantation that was marked by a sagging barbed wire fence. Hardy tromped down on the top wire while Jabo swung his leg over. They continued across what was once a pasture, now grown over with blackberry briars and weeds.

Hardy walked several yards in front of his father, the dogs roaming far ahead in search of quail. He stopped and looked back at Jabo plodding along.

"You okay?"

"Just taking my time."

After Jabo caught up with Hardy, they walked to the bottom of a steep hill then slowly climbed toward the ridge. Jabo's breathing was labored when he reached the top.

They rested a moment then spread out and made their way slowly across the field.

"Oughta be quail out there," Jabo said.

Hardy stepped lightly through the knee-high, brown sedge grass. A southpaw, he had his .16 gauge Remington cradled in the crook of his right arm. Jabo walked to his left. The dogs ranged in front, back and forth, their noses to the ground. The setter abruptly stopped and her tail stiffened. The whelp also stopped, then crept forward.

"Whoa, there!" Jabo commanded the pointer. He looked over at his son. "That bitch is gonna flush them birds sure as hell."

The pointer halted several feet behind the older dog and froze—tail stiff, one foot lifted, ears forward—a perfect point.

"I'll be damned," Jabo said begrudgingly. "She may turn out all right yet."

Hardy looked at the broad smile on his father's face.

"Let's flush 'em," Jabo said.

Hardy shouldered his Remington. The quails rose with a great muffled flapping of bronze wings reflecting the morning sun. He fired three times and one bird fell. He hadn't heard his father's gun. He looked over and saw the Browning slowly sliding from Jabo's arms to the ground. His father's hands reached for his chest as he crumpled forward.

"Hardeee..."

Hardy set down his gun and ran to his father's side. Jabo lay on the ground, vomit bubbling from the corner of his mouth.

"My God!" Hardy turned his father over and cradled his head in his arms. "Pop, what's wrong?"

"My chest...hurts."

"S-h-h-h. I'll get you outta here."

"I'll never…make it."

"Don't say that. I'm going for help." Hardy was panicking.

"No. Listen…"

"We shouldn't have come up here."

"Something you need…to know."

"Don't talk. Save your energy. I'm going for help."

"Leave it be…" Jabo's voice faded to a whisper. He coughed and groaned.

"What? What do you mean, leave it be?' Com'on, Pop. You're going to be all right. Just hang on."

✳   ✳   ✳   ✳

"James Bowman Jackson—Jabo to his friends—departed this earthly life day before yesterday," the Rev. Cletis Teeter intoned. "He died doing what he loved most—quail hunting. He was seventy years of age when the Lord took 'im.

"Jabo is survived by his son, James Hardy Jackson, his daughter-in-law, Millie, one grandson, Clint, and a host of relatives and friends. Let us pray."

Hardy shifted on the hard wooden pew at the Sweetwater Creek Baptist Church, wrapped his arms around Millie and Clint and bowed his head. Reverend Teeters prayed long and hard. Afterwards, Sheriff Pascal Horsely and The Lyrical Lawmen sang "Going Down the Valley" from the back of the sanctuary.

Hardy thought about what his father had said. How he kept muttering, "Leave it be, leave it be." The old man must have been delirious from lack of oxygen. There were so many other things left unsaid—like I love you. What was this unfinished business that ate his last breath?

In tiny Jackson Cemetery Jabo was laid to rest beneath the boughs of a white oak tree and alongside his wife of fifty years.

Inside the rusty, wrought iron fence were the graves of Hardy's ancestors. It was said that the Jacksons were all strong-willed people. His grandfather had sailed to France with the famed 42nd Rainbow Division during WWI. His great-grandfather, for whom he was named, had ridden with General Nathan Bedford Forrest during the War Between the States, and his triple great-grandfather had fought the British in Virginia.

The VFW chaplain, a grizzled veteran of WWII, stood over the open grave and recalled how Jabo had served his country. Then an honor guard of seven from the American Legion post fired three volleys into the gray sky over Jabo's coffin. A bugler played the long, mournful notes of taps.

And Hardy, pulling out a clean white handkerchief for a quick swipe at his eyes, realized that there was a lot about his father he didn't know.

CHAPTER 3

▼

"Judge Fagan called."

"What did the old warthog want?"

"Your presence in court!" his law partner, Sarah, said, voice tightening.

Hardy scissored the cordless phone between head and shoulder and propped his feet on the corner of the coffee table, strewn with an empty coffee cup, toast crumbs and dog-eared copies of *Writer's Digest*. "For what?"

"The Vebbert arraignment."

"Shit! I completely forgot about it." Hardy shot up from the couch.

"Obviously."

"You've got to cover for me." Hardy paced the den floor and massaged his forehead. "Millie kept me awake all night hacking and coughing. When I finally went to sleep it was early morning, and I overslept."

"Hardy, I know you've lost your dad and Millie's been sick, and I'm really sorry. But I've covered your ass for the last time. You spend more time plotting the 'Great American Mystery Novel' than you do worrying about the practice."

"Just one more time and I won't ever ask again. Okay?"

The line went dead. Hardy managed a tiny smile. Sarah Dickerson-Dunnivant was rougher than a cob, and he was lucky to have her.

* * * *

It was past 10 a.m. and skies were already iron gray when Hardy swung the Jeep Wagoneer wide on Joe Wheeler Street and U-turned into the handicapped space in front of his office. Parked in his usual spot was an old dark blue Ford van. The rear was smashed. He hoped the occupant was inside his office waiting to see him. Rear-end cases were money in the bank.

Hardy hung his coat on a hall tree in his small, dark-paneled, windowless office and buzzed Tommye Ann, his secretary.

"What's shak'in?"

"It's about time you showed up," she whispered. "These folks've been waiting on you almost an hour."

"Tell 'em I've been in court."

"Hardy, the lies I hav'ta tell for you will buy me a ticket to hell."

"What do they want?"

"They've been in a bad wreck," she whispered.

"I'll be right out."

* * * *

"We need to talk."

Hardy, lost in his book plot, looked up from the legal pad resting on his legs. Sarah stood in the doorway, case file clutched in one hand, the other on her hip. Short and slender as a reed, probably less than a hundred pounds, she was attired in her usual black flats, white socks, ankle-length skirt and white blouse. She was not happy.

"Come in. How did the arraignment go?" Hardy laid the pad on the desk, face down.

"Judge Fagan set the trial for December. And don't ask me to try it," she said flatly, pitching the file on his desk.

"That bitch will stick it to my client, and you know it."

"I find her to be very fair."

"Sure, if you're a woman. She slam-dunks my ass every time I go before her."

"That's because you represented her husband in their divorce."

"How did I know she would go to law school and get elected judge?"

"Karma?"

"Sit down and take a load off."

"I don't want to sit." She glanced scornfully at his feet on the desk. "Would you mind moving your feet. I want to talk to your face, not the soles of your shoes."

"Sorry." Hardy lowered his feet to the floor.

Sarah crossed her arms over her chest. "Hardy, this arrangement isn't working."

"Now, there you go. You said that three years ago and we're still together."

"Only because I have the patience of Job."

"Now don't get Biblical."

"Dammit!" Her brown eyes blazed.

"Well, sometimes people's hormones get out of whack. You oughta know that."

She stared unblinking at Hardy. "Hardy, you can be a real pig, and you'll never change. Why I ever agreed to practice law with you I'll never know."

"Mama loved me."

"You aren't pulling your load financially. I've got a kid I'm responsible for. I need to earn some money."

"How's Jasmine doing?"

"Don't change the subject."

"Joe not paying support?"

"Claims he lost his job. Probably quit. He just isn't dependable—unlike you, of course."

"I've got a few extra bucks you can have."

"Thanks, but no." She eyed Hardy. "This time I'm leaving."

"Come on, Sarah, don't talk like that." He got up and walked around the desk behind her chair and massaged her shoulders. "You've been working too hard," he said.

"I'm not changing my mind," she said, shrugging irritably out from beneath his big hands.

"You're right," Hardy said. "I haven't been pulling my load, especially since Pop died. I can't even bring myself to go over to his house. Too many memories."

"But it isn't Jabo's passing, Hardy. Let's face it. We're different. I came from Legal Services, you from the DA's office. You're a Republican; I'm a Democrat. You're Baptist; I'm Unitarian…"

"Full-service office."

"I must have been out of my mind," Sarah snorted.

He straightened the collar of her blouse.

"Been working on your novel again?"

"Just jotting down a few thoughts."

"Why do you waste time writing trash when you could earn money practicing law?"

"Law is boring."

"I like to eat."

"Cheer up. I signed up a rear-ender while you were in court. Whiplash."
She turned and looked up at Hardy.
"Honest?"
"Liability is clear and the injuries are serious."
"Insurance?"
"Money in the bank. Now cheer up."
Sarah sighed.

Chapter 4

Switzerland, November, 1995.

The black Mercedes snaked its way up the mountain. Hermann Blucker sat stiffly in the backseat, silver-headed cane between his knees. A light snow powdered the narrow road. In the distance, the village of Grindenwald twinkled in the night, and beyond was the larger Interlaken.

Behind the wheel was Heinz Quackernack, once a Uterschargfuhrer of an SS guard detail at Dachau. Riding shotgun was his identical twin, Hansel, also former SS. Both were large, bald men with powerful arms and thick necks. The only way Blucker could distinguish them was Hansel's notched right ear where a chunk had been shot away during the war.

Blucker was running late. Usually, he was as punctual as a Swiss train, but tonight he had doubled back to be sure he wasn't being followed.

He tapped his cane on the floorboard. "Heinz."

"*Ja,* Herr Blucker."

"A little faster, but carefully."

Heinz pressed the accelerator and the car lunged forward.

At a chalet nestled in a spruce grove, Heinz turned in and parked behind a row of BMWs and Mercedes. Hansel opened the back door for Blucker.

"You and Hansel remain with the car," Blucker said. "And keep your eyes open."

"*Ja.*"

Blucker pulled his gray topcoat around his tall, thin frame and lifted a leather briefcase from the trunk. He hobbled on his cane through snow to the chalet.

Inside, a group of men, all in their seventies, stood in front of a stone fireplace, chatting and drinking beer. When Blucker entered, they fell silent and raised their right arm stiffly.

"Heil Hitler!"

"Heil Hitler," Blucker returned.

Blucker moved among them, greeting each with a warm word and handshake.

"We must get down to business," he said. The men, clutching beer steins, moved to a circular table and stood quietly behind eleven chairs. Blucker took his position at the table beneath a large, red banner with a black swastika in a circle of white that hung on the wall.

"First, the oath." Blucker turned and faced the red and black banner. The men extended their arms in the Nazi salute and repeated the sacred oath—the oath each had taken when inducted into the SS more than fifty years ago and on every April 20th, when they met on Hitler's birthday.

> *I swear to thee Adolf Hitler,*
> *As Fuhrer and Chancellor of the Germany Reich,*
> *Loyalty and Bravery.*
> *I vow to thee and to the superiors*
> *whom thou shalt appoint*
> *Obedience unto death, So Help me God.*

The men lowered their arms.

"Believe! Obey! Fight!" Blucker said, repeating the SS slogan.

"Believe! Obey! Fight!" the men roared in response.

"Be seated, please."

The old men scraped back their chairs and sat around the table. Clearing his throat and adjusting his glasses, Blucker began, "Kamerads, the midnight hour approaches. A new day is about to dawn on Germany."

All nodded.

"Our Fuhrer is dead, but his dream still lives in the hearts and minds of many Germans and others of like persuasion around the world. We twelve men are the trustees of that dream. It is an abomination that we must meet under the cover of darkness. That will soon change. Our work and patience over the years have paid dividends. Our coffers are growing, our organization is strong and our will is undaunted. Sons of the Reich, take heart and prepare yourselves for the day. It is near. The people are ready for a change. The Fatherland is restless. Hoards of filthy foreign scum flood across our borders and defile our communities. They feed off the public dole like jackals on a carcass, not shedding a drop of sweat in return for our hospitality. The cost of caring for these aliens is enormous. Unemployment is rising. Crime is rampant. Germans are afraid to walk their streets.

The Jews have their heel on the neck of the masses. People cry out for leadership and order. Yes, order! Our once proud race is being mongrelized, our culture debased and our youth corrupted." Blucker's voice rose to a crescendo. "Our Fatherland must be saved! Our Fatherland will be saved!"

"*Ja—Ja.*"

"We must not fail. We will not fail." Blucker looked around the table at the men who sat motionless, listening. "Our secret has remained safe for fifty years. Now, that we are on the verge of implementing our plan, we must take every precaution to ensure that it remains secret. Timing is crucial. It is, my kamerads, a matter of life and death."

Willy Gleck, a bespectacled businessman from Munich who once commanded a Waffen SS Division, spoke up. "What about the Fuhrer document? Is there any indication of its whereabouts?"

"The document poses a great threat to our plan," Blucker said, looking to his left where Klaus Kluge sat, his arms folded across an ample chest. Kluge had commanded an SS guard detail at Stalag Luft VII near Bankau. He was tall and blue-eyed with a prominent nose and strong chin, his thin hair was slicked straight back. A black eye patch covered his left eye socket, the result of a Schrapnel fragment during the Battle of Berlin. But Kluge's most striking feature was an ugly scar that zigzagged down his left cheek and ended at a dimple in his chin, the result of a fencing mishap at the university.

"Klaus, what progress have you made since your last report in locating the missing Fuhrer document?"

"Not much," Kluge said. "We know, of course, that both the French Second Armored Division and the American 101st Airborne were in the Berchtesgaden area during the last days of the war. The French, I have eliminated from consideration. That leaves the Americans. The 506th Regiment of the 101st Airborne was given the mission of taking Eagles Nest, but military records are vague regarding who or what companies entered the bunker. Apparently, the soldiers scattered everywhere, looting."

"It is imperative that we locate the document," Blucker said.

"*Ja,*" Kluge agreed. "But it is quite possible that it no longer exists. Fifty years have passed and it has not surfaced. I have a roster of the men who served in the 506th Regiment. They have been watched as closely as possible under the circumstances. Many are now dead. I have also monitored their reunions, hoping to glean information. None has surfaced. Close watch has been kept of collectors of German military memorabilia. Nothing." Kluge held up his hands. "I have done all I know to do. I say the document no longer exists. Otherwise, it would have already appeared."

"Redouble your efforts," Blucker said. "It is a matter of utmost importance."

"*Ja.*" Kluge frowned.

Blucker looked around the table at Wilhelm Glickman, a stooped-shouldered man with long, angular face. He was vice-president of the Swiss National Bank in Interlaken. He had acted as go-between for the SS and the Swiss banks.

"Has there been any activity in the account?" Blucker asked.

"*Nien.* The account is quiet."

"There is danger in every operation," Deiter Krebs, a former Gestapo officer, interjected. "Since the document hasn't surfaced in fifty years, I agree with Klaus. It probably doesn't exist. I say we proceed with our plan."

Blucker looked across the table at the men. A few nodded their heads in agreement. The majority sat stone faced.

"*Nien.* It is far too risky," Blucker said. "First, we redouble our efforts to locate the document. No stone is to be left unturned. Possibly, our friends in America can help. But we must work fast. April 20th is fast approaching."

Blucker stooped over and lifted the briefcase to the table in front of him, then reached in his pocket and extracted a slender key. "I have a small present for you." He opened the case and brought out an 8-by-10 photo, holding it up for all to see. "As you can see, the Raven has turned out quite handsomely." He passed the photo around the table. The men leaned close to one another, eyeing the picture with obvious satisfaction. After everyone had seen the photo, Blucker walked to the fireplace and threw it in the flames.

"Now, let us drink to the future of the Fatherland," Blucker said.

"Here-here." They raised beer steins and someone began singing *Horst Wessel.* Everyone joined in lustily.

Chapter 5

Hardy looked around the stuffy, stale-smelling kitchen, a lump rising in his throat. He'd been dreading this. An egg yolk-encrusted plate sat on the table next to an empty coffee cup and nearby was an ashtray overflowing with cigarette butts. It seemed only yesterday when he would run in the backdoor, cut himself a piece of chocolate cake, then dash out to play. His chest tightened and he inhaled raggedly. Hell, he was alone, who was he hiding from? Tears streamed down his cheeks and he wiped them away with the back of his hand.

He walked down the hallway and lowered the thermostat, then emptied the garbage and arranged the dirty dishes in the washer. Afterwards, he searched for his father's will.

First, he looked in the den where Jabo usually kept his mail and monthly bills. He rifled through the stack of papers in the drawer—utility bill, credit card statements and a mail order application for cancer insurance, but no will. He looked through the gun cabinet, then on the mantle, below a large color print of Bo Jackson surging over the goal line in the 1982 Auburn-Alabama game.

In the living room, among the 50s-era furniture he searched end table drawers and under the couch and chairs. Nothing but dust.

He moved to the bedroom. The sheets on the bed were thrown back, as though his father had just climbed out. He searched through drawers, closet and even under the bed. Nothing. He did the same in all rooms. Jabo had always been secretive as an old maid, keeping his business to himself. There was no telling where his will was or even if he had left one.

In the garage, a rope dangled from a pull-down door in the ceiling. He had never been in the attic before. Jabo just said there was a bunch of old lumber stashed up there. He reached up and pulled the door down, unfolding the wooden ladder. He slowly climbed the rungs to the top and poked his head into darkness. Groping overhead, he found a string connected to a drop-cord and pulled. He climbed into the dimly lit attic where old plastic-shrouded clothes hung from a wire stretched from wall to wall. Cardboard boxes labeled "Christmas decorations" and old newspapers, magazines and broken furniture cluttered the room. His mother had never thrown anything away. Most of the stuff could go to the Salvation Army. He picked his way carefully across the creaky, cluttered floor. Cobwebs stuck to his face and he jerked back, swiping them away. In the shadows of a far corner sat a trunk. He walked over and stood a moment staring down at the trunk, then knelt and wiped the dust from the top. Stenciled on the olive drab lid were Jabo's name and serial number and a big lock hung from the hasp. With dust caked in the hinges and cobwebs covering all, it didn't appear to have been moved in years.

He lifted one end. Heavy. More of the junk he'd have to eventually clear out of this place when he got it ready to sell.

*　　*　　*　　*

At the car lot, Hardy searched through the mobile home and found nothing of importance except a safe deposit box key hanging on a nail with dozens of car keys. He drove to First National Trust where Jabo banked.

Nadine Booker, the bank's oldest employee, greeted him from behind a desk near the vault. "Bless yo' heart, I just can't get over yo' daddy pass'n. He wuz such a fine man and back before the war, one of the best dancers in the county. Oh, I could just go on forever talk'n about 'im."

"Yes, ma'am, thank you."

"Knowed 'yo mama, too. She wuz a Turner from 'cross the river, wasn't she?"

"Yes, ma'am." He handed her the key.

"How's Millie and the family?"

"Millie hasn't been feeling well lately, but Clint's fine."

That ritual out of the way, she pulled out an index card, held it close to her glasses and examined it, satisfied that his name was on the account.

"Just sign here," she said.

He followed her into the vault, where she located and unlocked the box and left him to his privacy.

Hardy pulled out a small metal box and set it on the shelf and examined its contents. There was an Army discharge, tax receipts, birth certificate, house deed, lease on the car lot and old monthly mortgage notes marked "paid in full," but no will and no insurance policy. There was a copy of a recent mortgage Jabo had taken out for $10,000. Hardy was surprised that his father was indebted. On second thought, he shouldn't be. Jabo had done nothing but drink and hunt for years.

It appeared he'd have to administer the estate through probate, and that meant obtaining a surety bond and filing an inventory of the personal property. Counting and listing every knife, fork and spoon would be a pain in the ass.

Chapter 6

▼

The green BMW glided quietly down the county blacktop west of French Springs, its high beams slicing through the moonlit night. Beethoven's Fifth reverberated from the speakers. Rudy Birch tingled with anticipation. Near the forks of the river, where the Elk flows into the Tennessee, he glanced a final time in his rearview mirror. He saw only the moon rising over the pines and leafless hardwoods. He turned left onto a narrow, gravel road to an A-frame cabin near the bank of the Tennessee River.

He parked behind the cabin, killed the engine and lights and looked around. Several hundred yards to the west lights from a neighbor's cabin window winked through the undergrowth and trees. Grabbing a bottle of Dom Perignon by the neck he slid out of the BMW and hurried through the night to the cabin.

Inside, he felt his way through the darkness and closed the blinds, then turned on a nightlight. He filled a silver bucket with ice and twisted in the bottle of Dom. Music. He loaded Beethoven into the CD player, pressed a button and the aria from *Don Giovanni* burst forth. He turned up the thermostat, lugged in an armload of wood from the back porch and built a fire in the stone fireplace. Soon the room glowed with warmth. He went to the bathroom, brushed his teeth and gargled. Standing before the mirror, he brushed back his blonde hair, then opened the two top buttons of his black silk shirt. He looked damn good, despite having a few miles on him. Returning to the living room, he switched off the lamp, stood with his back to the fire and waited.

Shortly, headlights blinked through the blinds, and a car engine purred to a stop. A door slammed. Rudy ducked hurriedly into the bathroom for a squirt of breath freshener. There was a tap on the back door. He moved quickly and swung open the door. A young woman with dark hair stood shivering in the cold. The collar of her black topcoat was turned up against her slender neck.

She smiled, her red lips parting. "*Bonsoir*, can you spare a franc, *Monsieur*? Is that the way you say it?"

Rudy laughed. "It's a dime, Claudette, my darling. Please come in from the cold." He ushered the young woman into the room lit only by the fire.

"Let me take your coat."

The young woman obliged as Rudy slid the coat from her thin shoulders, nuzzling the back of her neck.

"Hmmmm, you smell good."

"*Merci*. It's De Cartier you brought me," she said, turning to face him.

"And you look gorgeous." His eyes swept her fine-boned body, savoring every inch.

Claudette glanced around nervously.

"Relax. We're safe," Rudy said.

"What about…?"

"Sylvia?"

"*Oui*."

"She's Christmas shopping."

He went to the ice bucket and lifted out the champagne.

"Dom Perignon, 1975. The best—for us." He peeled off the wrapper, untwisted the wire and popped the cork. He poured the flutes half full.

"*Mademoiselle*, to a wonderful evening with a beautiful lady."

She nodded wordlessly.

They tapped rims and sipped the champagne. Rudy took her glass from her and set both flutes on the mantle. She cocked an eyebrow inquisitively, but didn't have to wonder long. He traced the creamy swells of her breasts and up to her neckline. There he hooked a finger under the fabric and eased it from her shoulder.

"God, you're so soft," he breathed in her ear.

He began to tug the dress. "Wait," she whispered, and turned her back to him. Rudy slid the zipper down over her firm, rounded backside and reached up to pull her dress down to her hips, where it dropped the rest of the way to pool on the floor at her feet. She slipped out of black suede pumps and left them nested in the circle of silky fabric.

She shivered before him in wispy black lace panties and bra. He reached for her and pulled her close.

"Cold?"

"No. No. It's just the way you look at me. It scares me sometimes."

"And what is it you think I'm going to do?" Rudy's fingers trailed up her spine and unhooked her bra quickly and expertly. Her beautiful breasts slipped free of their lacy bonds. He bent to take each of her nipples in turn into his mouth.

She pulled his head tightly to her, fingertips entwined in his thinning hair, stroking his scalp. He continued to flick his tongue in a circular movement between her breasts and down her belly, into and around her navel, while his fingertips worked under her panties.

He slid her panties down and dove greedily for the secret feast. She opened and he gripped her, pressing her ever closer to his searching mouth.

The young woman rolled her hips against him, imploring, pleading incoherently as he lowered her slowly to the braided rug in front of the fireplace.

* * * *

Sylvia Birch didn't consider herself insecure. But there were some things a woman had to know. She slowed the black Lexus and switched off the headlights. Near the gravel road to the cabin, she pulled onto the shoulder and parked. She climbed out of the car, closing the door softly, lifted a wool toboggan from her parka, pulled it down over her ears, and tucked her blonde hair beneath. In the distance the river gently lapped the shore. In hiking boots and jeans, flashlight ready, she inched her way along the edge of the woods until she reached the rear of the cabin. Two cars were parked in back—Rudy's BMW and a smaller car she didn't recognize.

Her heart plummeted. She had an inkling for some time that Rudy was unfaithful, but until this moment, had refused to believe it.

How could he? She leaned trembling against a tree, rage eclipsing her pain. "Two-timing shitheel," she gasped. She stumbled in the darkness, sobbing, her chest hurting while she searched for a stick to smash a window. She saw the gray outline of a dead limb on the ground, snatched it up and went for the bedroom window. She hesitated. Maybe she had jumped to the wrong conclusion. She dropped the stick and crept over to the light colored Honda Civic, and committed the tag number to memory. She couldn't think of anyone who drove such as car. She squatted, depressed the stem and let air from a front tire.

She moved quietly to the side of the cabin, pressed her ear against the shaded window, and listened. Music. *Don Giovanni*. A sliver of dull light escaped around the drawn blind. She cocked her head and tried to see inside.

She tiptoed onto the back porch and tried the door. Locked. She grimaced and swore under her breath. Creeping off the porch, she patted the ground until she found a rock, then crept back onto the porch. The door had a deadbolt. One quick blow against the glass pane and she could reach inside and twist open the lock. But what if there wasn't a woman? She'd look like a fool and her marriage would be over. Be smart, be smart. She had to know who was in the cabin. Eventually, whoever it was would have to leave. She would wait. She held her wrist to her face and squinted at her watch, an Ebel that Rudy had bought her in Switzerland. Eight-thirty. It could be a long night. It was cold. She pulled the parka snugly around her and thrust her hands into her pockets.

The wooded area between their cabin and the neighbors' was overgrown with briars and bushes, but the trees were large and offered a place to hide. Finding a large pine, she stood behind it and waited. The night was quiet. And cold. Real cold. Her toes were already numb. She stamped her feet to keep the circulation going.

"Shit! I'm freezing," she whispered.

She couldn't stand still. Walk around, she told herself. Her foot landed on something hard. It broke with a loud crack. A dog barked in the distance. She stood motionless. The dog barked again, then again. The back porch light of the cabin came on and Rudy stepped out and looked around for a moment, then went back inside. She had to get out of here. The dog was barking like a demon.

Sylvia bolted and ran down the road toward her car. She heard the dog barking behind her, getting nearer, closing in. Had she locked the car door? She prayed God she hadn't. Reaching the end of the road, she ran for the car, key in hand. The dog was nearly on her heels. She grabbed the door handle. Pulled. It opened. Thank God! She scrambled inside and slammed the door shut just as a Doberman reared against the window, fangs flashing.

Sylvia sat back in the seat, her heart pounding, and took a deep breath. When she stopped trembling, she fired up the Lexus and sped away.

Chapter 7

Sunny Webber drained the last drop of Chardonnay and set the crystal goblet on the side of the sunken black tub. She slid low into the hot bubbly water, rolled her neck on the curved headrest and closed her eyes. She really didn't have much time, but oh, God, it felt so good. Cocktails at 6 and dinner at 7:30, then the awards. The rumor was that she was on the short list. A tingling sensation raced through her body, then the butterflies returned. The wine sanded off the rough edges. She let her eyes drift open and gazed through the one-way glass that formed a wall in her spacious bathroom. A long, dark valley tapered down from the house to the Tennessee River. The sun had set, and in the west the lights of Huntsville glowed in the damp chill.

She stepped out of the tub and toweled off, critically examining her reflection in the mirror. Not bad for 55. Thank God for good genes and that doll-baby plastic surgeon.

She flicked on the bathroom TV. Peter Jennings was signing off on the evening news. She must hurry. Wrapping herself in a Chinese silk robe, she plopped down at the vanity, spritzed on some mouse and finger-combed her hair. After carefully applying makeup, she threaded on smoky pantyhose, then slipped into a black crepe dress with simple lines that fell to mid-calf. She fastened a single strand of pearls around her neck and inserted a single matching pearl in each earlobe.

She stopped for a final quick check in the foyer mirror, then slipped into a full-length mink coat, the silk lining cool against her bare arms.

Outside, she slid into her pinkish Lincoln Town Car, her trademark, lit the last cigarette in the pack, and headed down Monte Santo Mountain. At a gas station near the bottom of the mountain she pulled up to the glass front and honked her horn and lowered her window.

A man walked out of the service bay, rubbing his hands on a blue rag. Seeing the pink Town Car, he smiled and threw up his hand.

"Hi, Miss Sunny. What canna do for yuh?"

"Sam, would you mind getting me a pack of cigarettes?"

"Virginia Slims, right?"

"You haven't forgotten."

The man got her pack of cigarettes and she handed him a five.

"Keep the change, Sam. How's Nellie and the kids?"

"Just dandy, Miss Sunny." He looked in the car window at her. "You're sure doodied up this evening."

"Thanks. I'm going to the Charity Ball."

At the Von Braun Center, Sunny stood outside in the cold and took several quick drags on a cigarette, flipped it into the holly bushes, then went inside.

The banquet hall was noisy and filled to capacity. A young man in a black tux escorted her to a table near the front.

*   *   *   *

Special Agent Hank Duckworth sat hunched inside a gray Ford van, parked on a side street near Sunny Webber's house. He adjusted his headset and checked the remaining tape. The recorder was voice activated and hardly any tape had been used since he came on duty at 0700 hours. He got down on the carpeted floor on his haunches and did a few knee bends, rubbed both thighs then did head rolls and massaged the back of his neck with his hand. Nothing interesting had transpired since he placed the tap on Webber's phone three days ago. Tomorrow the van would have to be relocated before someone in the neighborhood became suspicious that it wasn't really a cable company doing repairs. Hearing a car pull up and stop, he parted the rear curtains and watched as Agent Preston hurried toward the van. He unlocked the back door and pushed it open. Preston climbed inside.

"It's about time," Duckworth growled.

"Sorry, but I got stuck in traffic."

Duckworth grimaced and pulled off the headset and entered the time in a logbook.

"Any activity?" asked Preston, positioning the headset.

"One of her agents called at 1710 hours and reported that she had an offer on a house on Tannohue Drive. The subject called a florist shortly thereafter and ordered flowers for someone in the hospital."

"Not much," said Preston.

"Well, it's all yours. I'm out of here. See you in the morning."

*   *   *   *

"Good evening ladies and gentlemen. Welcome to the twenty-fifth Charity Ball." The mayor adjusted her rimless glasses and looked out across a sea of beaming faces. It was Huntsville's premier black-tie event of the year. She cleared her throat and continued.

"It is my honor to introduce the recipient of the Golden Loaf Award. But first, let me remind you what the award represents. Providing for those who cannot care for themselves is the highest and noblest calling of mankind. Food for the hungry is at the top of the list. A loaf of bread has been designated as the symbol of United Charities since its beginning over twenty-five years ago.

"I know you're anxious to learn who this year's recipient is. The honoree has been actively involved in every facet of our community from the Red Cross to the Downtown Committee; from Neighborhood Watch to the Beautification Board; from United Givers to Heart Drive chairman. She is a successful businesswoman." A smattering of applause erupted from some women in the audience.

"Yes, the honoree is a woman. The owner of her own business, she epitomizes what a positive attitude can accomplish in this great country. Born in Germany in the cauldron of war, where many of her family members perished, she came to Huntsville as a nine-year-old. That was in 1950. She raised herself by her own boot straps. Actually, in her case it was spike heels. Beginning in real estate sales, she rose to president of her own company. We know it as Sunshine Realty."

Applause erupted and the audience came to its feet.

"None other than our own indomitable Magdalene "Sunny" Webber."

The band struck up "Sunny Days Are Here Again" as Sunny, radiant and smiling, made her way to the podium.

Chapter 8

Ben Wasserman's major interest in life was prosecuting Nazi war criminals. Five inches of snow and a rotten head cold would not stop him. He guided the black Volvo up Pennsylvania Avenue, past the homeless huddled in office doorways in ragged blankets and toward the Capitol. He moved at a snail's pace while tuned into NPR's *Morning Edition*. The big news was the budget stalemate between the President and Congress. And of course, the weather. More snow was expected.

Ben had seldom missed a day's work since coming on with the Office of Special Investigations in 1990. He tried to remember where he had stored his cross-country skis. His right leg was a barometer of the weather, thanks to his Jeep striking a landmine in Vietnam. This morning it hurt like hell. He had a lot of work to do; he'd ski to the office if he had to—bum leg or not. At 9th Street he turned right and drove into the Department of Justice garage. He limped toward the elevator, his lanky six-foot frame leaning under the weight of a large, brown leather briefcase.

Ben flicked on the light and hung his scarf and parka on a brass hall tree. He was the first to arrive at work, as usual. A staff attorney's salary wasn't great—he could earn a lot more at one of the big downtown law firms—but helping locate and prosecute Nazi war criminals who had sneaked into the country illegally was compensation enough. Ben's father died at Auschwitz in 1945, clubbed to death by an SS guard for not removing his cap quickly enough.

Ben unloaded the magazines and newspaper clippings from the briefcase, spread them on his desk and flicked on his computer. In addition to his regular duties of investigating and prosecuting Nazi war criminals, he also kept track of Neo-Nazi activities in Germany.

He completed summarizing the *Der Speigel* articles and was about to begin *Der Stern* when the intercom buzzed. He snatched up the receiver.

It was Roberta, the department secretary. "Mr. Jaffe would like to see you in his office. Now."

Ben tensed. Jacob Jaffe seldom invited a staff attorney to his office just to chat. He replaced the receiver and lifted a scarred watch from his pants pocket, his only memento of his dead father, at one time a Berlin lawyer. By a stroke of fate, two days before trucks came to relocate Jews in the Wasserman neighborhood, Ben and his mother had been sent to the country to visit relatives. The watch had gone with them. Ben snapped open the gold cover. 10 a.m. He assembled the unfinished report, which wasn't due for another day. Was Jacob confused about the due date? Ben's head pounded and his leg hurt. He dug two Alka-Seltzers from his briefcase and gulped them down before limping down the corridor.

Ben paused to button his coat and straighten his tie, then pushed open the door leading to the director's outer office. Roberta, plump and fortyish, smiled at Ben from behind her workstation.

"Good morning, Mr. Wasserman."

"Hello, Roberta. I'm amazed you made it to work this morning."

She poked a booted leg from behind the desk. "I'm from Buffalo, remember? The blizzard capital of the country."

"How are the kids?"

Roberta made a face.

"Keep the faith. They're not teenagers forever."

"Thanks." She gestured with her head. "You can go on in."

Ben tucked the report under his arm, took a deep breath, pecked on the tall door and entered the room.

Except for his silver hair, Jacob didn't look sixty. Like most avid runners, he was lean and agile. Already up from his desk and halfway across the spacious room with hand extended, Jacob was smiling.

"Hello Ben. How are you?"

"Fine."

Jacob shook Ben's hand warmly, clasped his shoulder and squeezed. "You look tired."

"I've been trying to complete this report." Ben held up a sheaf of papers. "It's not due until tomorrow, you know."

Jacob nodded. "I know. Have a seat." He gestured toward a chair, then sat behind a desk cluttered with files and documents. On the credenza was an inscribed black and white photo of a younger Jacob shaking hands with JFK.

"What's the bottom line of your report?" Jacob asked.

"Same as usual. Neo Nazi's are working overtime."

Jacob creaked back in his chair. "Give me the details."

Ben cleared his throat and glanced at the report in his lap.

"In Potsdam, a teenage girl was stabbed in the face after she ignored a Nazi salute. In Lausanne, a home for asylum-seekers was torched by racists. A Frankfurt University professor denied the Nazi Holocaust. In Brandenburg, a seventeen-year-old anti-fascist was beaten by three fascists. That's all within a week. Jewish graves desecrated with swastikas and graves destroyed."

Jacob held up his hand. "I get the picture. As the journalist, Ben Hecht, wrote: 'The Germans have not reformed. They are resting.'"

"It does appear that way," Ben said.

Jacob leveled steel blue eyes on Ben. "I didn't invite you here to discuss the report. I have something else in mind." Jacob opened up a file on his desk and paged through it for a moment in silence. That's when Ben saw his name. It was his personnel file.

"You're getting a few gray hairs," Jacob said. "A good executive needs two things: gray hair and hemorrhoids. The former gives him the appearance of maturity and the latter causes him to sit up straight and pay attention."

Ben chuckled. "I qualify on both counts."

Jacob leaned forward, his slender hands clasped and resting on the desk. "How would you like to take on more responsibility?"

"My plate is already full."

"Perhaps, I should have said different responsibilities."

"If it's interesting."

"We have big fish to catch. The AG, for reasons I'm not at liberty to disclose at the moment, wants to create a new unit within OSI. I am recommending you for the job."

Ben allowed himself a tiny smile. "Thanks for the confidence. What's it about?"

"At the present time, I can't tell you exactly what your duties will be. The subject is so sensitive that only a few people outside the Oval Office know. Interested?"

"You bet."

"I thought you would be."

Chapter 9

Hardy sat in Dr. Jack Passman's waiting room, turning through dog-eared pages of a year-old *Field & Stream*. He twisted nervously in his chair. A door opened and Hardy looked up. Millie emerged holding a piece of paper. He jumped to his feet, waiting for her to speak, but she remained silent.

"Well, what did he say?"

"He wants me to have some tests tomorrow in Huntsville."

Hardy had a sinking feeling. Tomorrow? He held open the door for Millie as they left the doctor's office.

"Is that all he said?"

"Pretty much." She feigned a laugh. "You know how doctors are. They won't tell you anything."

* * * *

Hardy and Millie sat quietly on the black leather couch in Dr. Passman's private office two days later. Millie yawned nervously. Hardy leaned forward and cracked his knuckles and looked idly around the room, first at the framed print of a sailing vessel above the antique mahogany desk, then at the long row of medical volumes in the bookcase. A life-size human skeleton dangled from a stainless steel rod in one corner. He looked away.

"I hate the waiting part," he said.

Millie reached over and patted his hand. "I'll be okay, darling."

"Of course you will."

But Hardy was uneasy. He hated the antiseptic smell of the room. He said a silent prayer—the same one, over and over—"Please God don't let anything be wrong with her."

The door swung open and Passman walked in, wearing a white jacket and holding a paper.

Hardy took Millie's hand and studied Passman's solemn face. Millie's hand trembled.

Passman sat down behind his desk, placed the paper before him, looked up at Millie, cleared his throat and said quietly, "I'm afraid I have bad news."

Hardy's stomach turned over.

"Give it to me straight," Millie said, her voice quavering.

"Bronchogenic carcinoma. Lung cancer."

"Oh God!"

Hardy felt her hand go limp.

"It's treatable," Passman quickly added.

Chapter 10

▼

The attic was cold, but Hardy felt flushed. He unzipped his windbreaker and knelt in front of the trunk. The lock was a heavy-duty Yale. It made no sense to him to have to do this since he was the sole heir, but it was the law. Anyway, he was curious about what was in the footlocker since that day he first spied it shortly after Jabo died.

He pressed the hacksaw blade to the lock and sawed hard and fast. Steel rasped against steel.

When he sawed half way through the lock, he stopped and flexed his hand, then after a moment's rest, continued sawing. At last the blade sliced through the steel.

"There." He dropped the hacksaw.

He took the lock in his hand and twisted, but the hasp didn't budge. He'd have to cut the other side. He picked up the saw and went back to work. His heart was racing faster with each stroke of the blade. He shouldn't be doing this, no matter what the law required. "Leave it be," his father's repeated. Could it have been the footlocker he was talking about? It wasn't too late to walk away. He continued sawing. It was cold and his fingers were numb. Just as his hand gave out, the lock dropped to the floor with a thud.

He massaged his hands while eyeing the footlocker. He slowly lifted the lid and folded it back against the wall. A sweet, pungent odor stung his nostrils. Mothballs. He looked inside the trunk.

Army uniforms. He lifted out an olive-drab wool jacket with sergeant stripes on the shoulders, a row of ribbons was pinned over the left breast pocket. There were several pairs of faded fatigues with an eagle patch on the shoulder. A German pistol lay on top of an army blanket.

He pulled back one corner of the blanket.

"Good God Almighty!"

Hardy's mouth gaped wide. He stared at rows and rows of money, banded and neatly placed in the bottom of the trunk. He picked up a bundle of bills and tried to read what was written on the paper band. It was in German. A swastika was printed on the wrapper. He counted the bundles of bills, stacked two deep. There were ninety in all.

In the corner of the trunk was a small tobacco sack. He picked it up, loosened the strings, worked open the top and looked inside.

"My God!" He held the sack away at arm's length, repulsed by what he saw. Gold-filled teeth.

He noticed a white envelope in the bottom of the trunk. He picked it up and held it under the light, noting the fine quality of the paper. Embossed on the envelope were the initials "A.H." In the center of the letters was an eagle standing on a wreath encircling a swastika. One end of the envelope had been sliced open. He slipped out a document and unfolded it, careful not to tear the fragile creases. It was official looking with a seal imprinted at the bottom, but it was written in German and he couldn't read a word.

He refolded the document and slid it back into the envelope and placed it in the pocket of his windbreaker. Replacing the money and covering it with the blanket and clothes, he shut the trunk lid and stacked old magazines on top. He turned to leave, stopped, opened the trunk and dug down inside and pulled out a bill, and hid it in his wallet.

Chapter 11

▼

"I think my husband is seeing another woman," Sylvia Birch said, clutching a tissue.

"It can happen. I should know," Sarah said. Self-disclosure was a communication technique she had learned at a divorce workshop.

Sarah eyed the well-dressed blonde sitting across the desk. In her mid-thirties, tall and thin—almost too thin—she was wearing black crepe pants and matching top. Her large, blue eyes, filled with uncertainty, were red from crying.

The solitaire on her third finger was at least three carats. She was high maintenance. Good for at least a ten thousand retainer.

"Then you understand my situation," Sylvia said.

"Yes."

"I'm very nervous about being here."

Sarah flashed an understanding smile and set down her pen. "Take a deep breath and relax. We have plenty of time. I've been told I'm a pretty good listener."

"Do you know my husband, Rudy Birch? We live in Huntsville. He operates WorldWide Travel Agency."

Sarah searched her memory. She had never heard the name. "Noo...I don't think so."

"Good. And what I tell you is confidential?"

"Absolutely."

"I hardly know where to begin."

"At the beginning," Sarah said, "Or wherever you feel comfortable."

She took a deep breath and sat back in her chair. "I met Rudy three years ago on a trip to France. After my divorce some of my friends at the office were concerned about me, thought a trip would help. So they put it together and the next thing I knew I was flying off to Paris. Rudy was our tour agent. He swept me off my feet. He was—is—well, sexy. A year later, we married. He makes very good money. I quit work. I thought we had a good marriage. Then last week, I caught him with another woman at our river cabin." She dabbed away tears in the corner of her eye. "Please forgive me. I promised myself I wouldn't cry."

"I understand. Just take your time," Sarah said.

"I've lost fifteen pounds since I found out. I can't sleep or concentrate. I'm never hungry. One minute, I want to confront Rudy, the next, I don't want to know."

"Yes, I do," said Sarah. "Maybe you should see a counselor. It helped me."

"Maybe I should."

"Do you know the woman's name?" Sarah asked, poising her pen over a yellow pad.

"No. Actually I didn't go inside the cabin."

"Did you see the woman enter or exit the cabin?"

"Not really."

"Tell me exactly what you did see," Sarah said.

"A car parked in back that I wasn't familiar with." She reached into her purse and withdrew a scrap of paper. "And I heard music inside the cabin. I have the tag number of the car."

"Who's it registered to?"

"I don't know."

"Would you like for me to find out?"

"Yes, thank you." Sylvia handed the paper to Sarah. "Right now I would like to know my legal rights."

"If you divorce, you're entitled to an equitable share of the marital estate. That's property you and your husband have accumulated during the marriage."

"What about assets owned before the marriage?" Sylvia asked.

"They aren't considered part of the marital estate unless they have been commingled with marital assets." Sarah paused. "Do you have any idea how much assets we're talking about?"

"Heavens no!" Sylvia shook her head. "Rudy is close-mouthed."

"Don't you see your income tax returns?"

"Just the part I sign. He just tells me to sign at the bottom, and I do."

Sarah's brown eyes widened. "What about a joint bank account?"

"I have my own account into which Rudy makes weekly deposits. Where he banks or how much he earns is a mystery to me. We live in a nice home on Green Mountain. I drive a Lexus, wear nice clothes and have credit cards. Rudy is very attentive to my material needs. What about alimony?"

"You can ask for it, but it's discretionary with the court. Usually, one must prove fault on the party that caused the break-up."

"What should I do?" Sylvia asked.

"First get hard evidence that he's committing adultery."

"Do I have to catch him in the act?"

"No, just enough evidence to convince a person of guarded discretion that adultery is being committed. That's the test imposed by our Supreme Court. I would recommend you hire a PI."

"Rudy knows a lot of important people in Huntsville." Sylvia said. "Can we file in this county?"

"The proper venue is the county where the defendant resides. We can file here, but it's subject to being removed to Huntsville." Sarah grinned wryly. "If we can keep the case in this county, I believe our judge will respond favorably. She's a woman, and she's been through a divorce."

"How much is this going to cost me?"

"My retainer is ten thousand. When that's used up, you'll be billed monthly at a hundred and fifty an hour. All fees must be paid before any court appearance."

Sylvia reached in her purse and extracted a wad of hundred dollar bills and counted them out on Sarah's desk.

"I've been putting aside a little each week so that I could have money I didn't need to account for. Rudy keeps up with every penny I spend."

*　　*　　*　　*

Sylvia lay awake and still as death on her side in the king-sized bed, facing the bedroom wall, eyes closed. Rudy was in the bathroom blow-drying his hair, getting ready for work. She heard him spray on cologne, and seconds later the tangy scent wafted into the bedroom where she lay. He tiptoed from the bedroom and quietly closed the door.

Downstairs, a door slammed. The garage door raised and a car engine started.

Sylvia swung out of bed and went to the window, cracked the drapes and watched as Rudy backed out of the driveway. After the BMW rounded the corner, she slipped on her housecoat and went downstairs to the utility room that adjoined the kitchen. She opened a clothes hamper next to the washer and dryer, pulled the dirty clothes out onto the floor, then pawed through the pile until she found Rudy's beige silk boxers. She held them close and examined them. Seeing nothing of interest, she threw them on the floor and picked up another pair, his blue ones. A red smear was on the front. It appeared to be lipstick. Her heart sank and she stood trembling, not wanting to believe what she saw. She walked to the window and held the underwear in the light and looked again. No doubt about it. Lipstick. She sniffed the material. A trace of perfume lingered. She went to the kitchen, found a plastic sandwich bag and stuffed the soiled underwear inside, then zipped the bag shut. She tucked the package in her purse.

* * * *

"We sell more of these than anything in the store," the clerk said, lifting a black recorder from the display case for Sylvia to get a better look. "It's only $175 and easy to hook up." He paused. "Do you have an attic?"

"Yes."

"Good. Find the phone line that comes into the house. It'll be black. Peel back the insulation and you'll see two wires, one green, one red. Follow?"

Sylvia nodded. "Then what?"

"Peel back the insulation on the green and red, but don't cut them, okay?" He picked up another device. "Splice this phone jack into the green and red wires, plug the recorder into the jack and you're in business."

"What powers the recorder?"

"Batteries. It's voice activated."

"What about tapes?"

"You'll need to change every day or so. I'll throw in five to get you started."

The man rang up the purchase. "One more thing," he said and pointed to a hand-lettered sign on the wall behind the counter. "It's a violation of federal law to secretly record someone's phone conversation without their permission. We're not responsible, okay?"

* * * *

In her bedroom, Sylvia changed into jeans and pulled on a baggy sweatshirt. Strapping on a fanny pack containing the recording device, she went into the garage. The attic entrance was a small opening in the ceiling covered with a piece of plywood. She'd never been in the attic.

A ladder stood nearby. She positioned it under the entrance, climbed up and slid back the plywood, then hoisted herself into the attic. It was dark and cold. She found the light cord and gave a yank. Great heaps of cottony insulation lay between ceiling joists. On top was a narrow catwalk. Dozens of white wires criss-crossed the attic floor. Where was the phone line? Placing each foot on a 2-by-8 beam, she straddled the insulation and inched her way to the corner of the attic. A timber creaked. Startled, she looked to see if someone was in the attic. At the eave, she pulled back dusty insulation and felt for the phone line. It was an easy find. She sneezed and lifted a black wire. There had to be a more accessible location to connect the recorder. Perhaps near the attic opening. She lifted the wire above the insulation and followed it towards the opening. The wire was hung on something. She lifted. A black object dangled from the wire. Looking closer, she recognized a small tape recorder. Dropping the black line, she jerked back, almost losing her footing. She trembled. Who would do this? And why?

She carefully covered up the recorder.

Chapter 12

▼

Hardy let himself in the side kitchen door. Millie, in pink pajamas, sat at her piano softly playing Chopin. Aubie was asleep nearby. Hardy studied Millie. God, she looked awful. Every time she had chemo, she was sick for days. Her once thick hair had fallen out.

She looked up at him.

"Hi, sweetheart," he said softly.

"Darling, what are you doing home?" A tiny smile creased her wasted face.

"To check on my woman. What else?"

"I wish you would fix the commode off our bedroom. It won't flush."

"The chain is broken," he said.

He found the cordless phone and went into the bathroom, closed the door and sat on the commode lid. He took a deep breath, called information and got the number of the German Consulate in Atlanta. He punched them quickly before he forgot.

"*Guten Tag, hierspricht das Deutsche Konsulat. We kann ich ihnen helfen?*" a woman answered.

"Hi, this is Stan Jason," Hardy said. "I was rummaging through a trunk the other day and found some old German money and was wondering if it had any value."

"One moment, please," the woman said in English. "I'll switch you."

Hardy waited for what seemed an eternity. His mouth was dry and made a popping noise when he talked. A man picked up, "*Guten Tag.*"

Hardy repeated the story.

"What type of money is it?" The man asked in perfect English.

"Reichsmarks."
"No value whatsoever."
"What!"
"It is valueless, sir."
"Are you sure?"
"Quite positive. Well, it might have some value to a collector, but that's all."

Chapter 13

"Gentlemen, the Attorney General will see you," said the receptionist.

Ben rose and straightened and buttoned his gray pinstripe coat. "I'm nervous as hell and I don't know why," he whispered to Jacob.

"You'll do fine." He patted Ben on the back.

"Will you at least give me a clue?"

"Patience."

Jacob pushed open the tall door and ushered Ben into the AG's office. Behind the desk sat a rather plain-looking woman, with short hair and glasses. She was poring over a file. Glancing up, she closed the file, got up and came from behind the desk.

"Gentlemen, please come in." Her hand was extended toward Jacob. "It's good to see you."

"Thank you, Madame Attorney General, and likewise."

She shook Ben's hand firmly. "It's so nice to see you again," she said. "I was thinking this morning, I believe the first time we met was nineteen-ninety when I was still attorney general of Florida."

"Yes, that's correct," Ben said.

"Please be seated." She swept her arm toward two leather chairs positioned in front of her desk.

The two men sat in silence as the AG took her seat. She placed both hands on the chair arms.

She leveled her eyes on Wasserman. "As you know Ben, the decision has been made to create a special unit within OSI."

"Yes."

"Jacob has recommended you to head up the unit. I've reviewed your personnel file as well as your performance records and concur with his recommendations. The question in your mind at this time must be, what is this about?"

"Yes."

The AG leaned forward. "Ben, this matter is of the most sensitive nature. There are few people outside the Oval Office privy to this information. What you are about to undertake, if you should so decide, is of the utmost importance."

Ben tucked his chin, a surge of exhilaration shooting through his body.

"Allow me to explain. In the closing days of World War II as the Russians advanced from the east, many Germans fled west and surrendered to the Americans. The most significant of these was a group of Peenemunde rocket scientists who developed the V-1 and V-2 under the leadership of Werner Von Braun. They gathered near Hindelang, Bavaria, close to the Austrian border, waiting for the American forces. Contact was made by elements of the 324th Infantry Regiment, 44th Division. An agreement was made by our government to allow these scientists to come to the U.S. in return for their services in developing our rocket program. In September, Von Braun left for France then went to El Paso, Texas. Over the next few months one hundred twenty-seven of his co-workers went to Ft. Bliss, and later White Sands." The AG glanced down at the file.

Why was she telling him this, Ben wondered. He knew the story well. Anyone had access to this information.

The AG clasped her hands together and continued in a lowered voice. "We believe that a male child, whom I will call Raven, and posing as the son of one of the scientists, was brought into the country. That, of course, was illegal. It wasn't until the Berlin Wall was torn down and we gained access to East German Staats Sicherheits-Dienst records that we became aware this had happened.

"We are pretty sure the boy was sneaked into the country under forged documents. Once here, he was most likely given a new identity and sent to live with another family. He could be anywhere. We don't even know for certain if he's still in this country." She paused. "Any questions so far?"

"Just one," Ben said. "Why is it so important that we find this individual?"

The AG slouched and her eyes narrowed. "I can't reveal that information. At the risk of sounding melodramatic, let me say that the well-being of the free world may hang in the balance."

There was a long silence.

"The President wants someone dedicated to the mission, Ben." She glanced down at his personnel file. "I think you're that person."

"Yes. Yes, of course."

"Good!" The AG smiled and sat forward and said with a note of urgency, "Ben, you've got to find him before April 20th."

"April 20th!"

"Jacob can fill you in on the details of what little information we have. Ben, you will report directly to me, but keep Jacob informed of your progress. Any questions?"

The men looked at each other, then shook their heads. The AG glanced at her wristwatch and rose to her feet. "Well, gentlemen, in that case, I apologize for rushing you, but I'm due at the White House."

She shook Ben's hand. "Congratulations, Ben. You are now head of operations, Eagle's Talon. Good luck."

* * * *

In Jacob Jaffe's office, Ben had mixed feelings about what had occurred. A part of him was excited, another part apprehensive. What if he couldn't deliver?

"What about support?" Ben asked.

"You will have an investigator and historians assigned to the team."

"Only one investigator?"

"I have authorized two. We don't want to raise any eyebrows. As far as other OSI personnel are concerned, they will not be told your true mission. Your team will be sworn to secrecy."

Jacob unlocked a file cabinet and lifted out a thin folder and placed it on the desk before him.

"There isn't a lot of information available," Jacob said. "I'll tell you what I know. Of the one hundred twenty-seven scientists that Von Braun assembled in Bavaria, several of them had children. Here's a list." He handed Ben several sheets of paper. "In 1947, they moved to Huntsville, Alabama, where they worked in the space program and lead normal lives, becoming U.S. citizens in 1954."

"Before they became citizens, was any effort made to keep track of their activities?"

"Not much. They worked hard at their jobs and made enormous contributions both to the community, and of course, to the nation. It is therefore imperative that you be very discreet in your investigation."

After Ben had perused the papers, he looked up and said to Jacob, "Is this all I have to go on?"

"I'm afraid so."

Chapter 14

▼

Wilhelm Glickman always arrived at the Swiss National Bank promptly at 8:50 a.m. But this morning he was late. And he was worried.

The lines in his long, angular face were deeper and more pronounced than usual. The reason was the headline on the bottom fold of the *International Herald Tribune*: "Nazi Fortune in Secret Swiss Account."

The train glided down the rails that skirted Lake Thunersee, screeching to a stop at Bahnhof West in Interlaken. Glickman stepped down from the passenger car into the cold morning, tucked the folded newspaper under his arm, and hurried down the sidewalk as quickly as his 78 years would allow. The leaden sky threatened snow. He tugged the brim of his black Homburg and buttoned his matching great coat to the top.

When he reached the three-story brownstone at 110 Rosenstrasse, he took the elevator to his second floor office. Inside, he shed his hat and coat and took a seat behind his desk, a handsome walnut with carved claw feet. He spread out the newspaper and reread the article, more slowly this time. It was the third such story in as many weeks. The first two had been hidden away inside the paper, but now the story had made the front page. Momentum was building, and that was bad news.

The article recounted the earlier British claims that "billions remain in secure and quiet Swiss bank vaults," estimating that $500 million was on deposit at the end of World War II, and at today's prices would be worth about $4 billion. Lawsuits filed by the World Jewish Congress had touched off public hearings by the U.S. Senate Banking Committee. This prompted the American president to create a commission to search for Nazi funds that might have ended up in U.S.

Federal Reserve vaults. Now Swiss politicians were feeling the pressure and were considering conducting an investigation to determine if any Nazi "Holocaust funds" were hidden in secret accounts.

Glickman folded the newspaper with trembling hands and slumped back. The more publicity, the more likely that someone might begin asking questions about a certain numbered account at Swiss National, which he managed personally. It had been initially opened in 1933, shortly after the Fuhrer had become Chancellor of Germany. Deposits had been made regularly, becoming larger as the war progressed, and by the time Germany surrendered in May 1945, the balance stood at well over 50 million Swiss francs. Through investments and inflation, the account was presently worth an estimated $900 million.

There was only one problem. No one could withdraw the money. The Fuhrer document, giving the bearer power of attorney to access the account, had been missing for fifty years.

*   *   *   *

It was noon when Glickman, thin shoulders hunched, exited the bank and walked briskly, but carefully, down the snow-slick sidewalk. At Bahnhofplatz, he turned south.

At the Shilthorn Hotel, a four-story white stucco that catered mostly to German tourists, Glickman knocked the snow from his shoes and entered the small lobby. Heinz Quackernack was behind the caged desk.

"*Wo ist Herr Blucker?*" Glickman asked.

Heinz pointed toward the small dining room just off from the lobby. "He is eating lunch."

Glickman found Blucker seated at a corner table, bent over a plate of noodles, a tall glass of beer crowned with an inch of foam in front of him. "Herr Blucker."

Blucker looked up from his plate and adjusted his glasses. Seeing his old comrade in arms brought a pleased look to his face.

"Herr Glickman, *mien* friend, what brings you out on such a snowy day?"

"Bad news."

"Sit."

Glickman peeled off his coat and draped it over a chair. From the pocket, he took the newspaper. "Have you seen this?"

Blucker glanced at the newspaper. His face grew rigid and his black eyes hardened. "*Ja*, I read it this morning. The media are like a pack of jackals the way they howl, but they will never goad Swiss politicians into conducting a meaningful investigation."

"I am worried," Glickman said. "What if the politicians cave into the pressure?"

Blucker tore off a chunk of black bread and paused with it in his gnarled hand. "They will not. It would tear this country apart. Too many powerful people have profited from Third Reich fortunes. The politicians will make noise, but they will not act. No kamerad, do not trouble yourself unduly. We must be quiet like the stag in the forest, quietly watching as the hunters pass by."

Glickman leaned back in his chair, some of the tension leaving his body. "*Ja*, perhaps you are right. Interlaken is such a small town and the bank is tiny compared to others in Switzerland."

"This was part of the grand design many years ago when the plan was conceived," Blucker said. Then he leaned over the table and said in a hushed tone. "The greatest threat to our plan is that someone will find the missing Fuhrer document before we do. Locating that document is imperative. We must find it!"

Chapter 15

Hardy sped toward Huntsville, Garth Brooks crooning on the radio. His thoughts were on the reichsmarks.

At a beige brick post office in West Huntsville, he waited in line while people in front bought stamps and money orders. Finally, his turn came and he stepped up to the window.

"Yessir. Can I hep'ya?" asked the clerk.

"I'd like to rent a box."

The clerk reached behind him, lifted a white card and slid it across the countertop. "Fill this out and turn it back in."

No I.D. was asked. Nothing. Hardy picked up the card, a snap out type with carbon copies, and went back to the Jeep. Using the steering wheel as a desk, he filled in the blanks. He looked vacantly in the distance, thinking about what he was doing. Across the street, a beer sign glowed in a dingy tavern window. A beer would knock off his nervous edge. He cranked and pulled across the street to Shirley's Lounge and parked on the pot-holed asphalt next to a dirty old Chevy with a bent fender and red mud-splattered tires.

Inside, Hardy looked around the dimly lit room. A heavyset blonde in jeans was sweeping cigarette butts and trash into a heap. Hardy went to the bar, ordered a Coors and rethought his plan. He examined the application once more to be sure he had filled in all the blanks.

"Ain't seen 'ya 'round here before."

Hardy looked down the row of bar stools to where a small, thin man in soiled khakis and grungy toboggan sat hunkered over a beer. He was shaking salt into the mug. He pinched a cigarette between yellowed fingers.

"That's right," Hardy said.

"I stay 'cross the street at the Mayflower," the man said. "It's the flagship of flop houses. I do my drank'n and socializing in here. Folks call me Doolittle."

Hardy nodded. "Glad to meet you. I'm uh… Joe…, Joe Smith. Like the Mormon leader."

"From 'round here?"

"Not exactly."

"Didn't think so." Doolittle sized up Hardy. "Ain't the law, are 'ya?"

"No."

"Didn't think so." Doolittle set the salt shaker down. "Yeah, I know most everybody in the neighborhood." He drained his beer.

Hardy turned to the woman sweeping and said, "Another beer for my friend." He got up and moved closer to Doolittle.

"Thanks, Joe," slurred Doolittle as he peered at him through glassy, bloodshot eyes.

"Think nothing of it."

The blonde slid a mug down the bar where it stopped in front of Doolittle.

"How would you like to earn some extra cash?" Hardy asked.

"Doin' what?"

"Picking up mail once a week and holding it for me."

"Ain't kiddie porn, is it?"

"No way!"

"Ain't drugs?"

"No. I just moved and don't want my wife nosing through my mail."

"Know what che' mean."

"Will you do it?"

"Sure."

Hardy thrust out his hand and the men shook.

Hardy lifted a ten from his wallet and shoved it in Doolittle's shirt pocket. "As soon as I get my box number, I'll be in touch."

* * * *

It was mid-morning and cold one week later when Hardy picked up two keys at the post office. He found Doolittle, sitting on a stool at Shirley's, bleary eyed from beer and smokes.

"Is there somewhere we can talk," asked Hardy.

"Sure, come on across to the Mayflower. My room ain't much, but it's private."

The pair entered Doolittle's room, and he was right. It wasn't much. Hardy tried not to look around and inhaled only enough to remain oxygenated. He needed to get this over quickly.

"Don't lose this." Hardy handed Doolittle a key to box number 1100. "Pick up my mail and I'll check in with you every week or so."

Doolittle said, "You know, I been thinkin' this deal over and it seems like to me you handin me a ten spot every now and then ain't much for runnin interference for ya. See'in how ya don't want your missus snoopin in this, it must be somethin a bit touchy, like maybe yore expectin a real personal message from someone. Don't get me wrong. It don't make no never mind to me if yore gittin a little on the side. When I wuz married I stepped out a little now and then myself. What I'm sayin is I know it's worth more to ya than yore offerin."

The old bastard was putting the squeeze on him. Hardy could fork over a few extra bucks, but if he caved in too easily, Doolittle would keep bleeding him. Sweat trickled down between his shoulders as the stale air began to close in on him. He shrugged out of his jacket and threw it over the back of a scarred desk chair.

"Let me think about it," said Hardy. "I've got to pee."

"Hep yerself," Doolittle said, jerking his head toward the bathroom.

The door banged shut behind Hardy, and swung back a few inches from its sprung latch. He ripped off a piece of tissue, gingerly lifting the lid of the stained toilet. When he finished, he stepped to the sink, which was stained nearly as bad as the crapper from cigarettes left to burn down on the edges. He rinsed his hands, glancing in the cloudy mirror over the sink and saw Doolittle bending over the desk. Hardy kept the water running and continued to watch the reflection of the old man as he lifted his jacket from where he tossed it and started going through the pockets. Doolittle found some loose change in a front pocket and stuffed it into his own. Next, he fished Hardy's wallet out of an inside pocket, flipped it open and was about to pluck out a bill when Hardy burst out of the john.

"What the fuck are you doing, old man? I told you I'd pay you for your services and I will."

Doolittle jumped and reeled, lost balance and staggered backward. Hardy grabbed for him and missed. Doolittle fell, and Hardy winced at the sound of bone striking the edge of the dresser.

Hardy leaped to his side and slid his hands under the limp, frail shoulders, sitting him up on the matted shag carpet.

"You all right, pops?"

"Yeah, I guess I'm all right. Ya understand don't you? I just needed a few bucks extra. They're about to throw me outta this place and I've had all of livin in a refrigerator carton that I can take, especially with winter comin on."

It was then that Hardy noticed a dark stain spreading on the back of Doolittle's collar.

"You're bleeding," said Hardy. Blood oozed from a gash in the back of Doolittle's head. "Let me help you on the bed."

He sat the old man on the edge of the bed and went in search of a clean wash cloth. He couldn't find anything remotely clean, so he pulled out a freshly laundered handkerchief from his back pocket and soaked it with cold water for a compress.

"There, hold that on your head until it stops bleeding."

"Thankee. I'll be all right. Gittin a little bit of a headache, but that might be from cheap wine. Heh, heh."

Hardy could see that the old man was dazed, but he seemed to be coming around. It was a mistake to get involved with the old drunk in the first place. He'd better keep looking for someone to check his box.

"I hope I still got the job...Smith?," pleaded Doolittle. "I need it bad, like I told ya. I promise no more funny stuff."

Reluctantly, Hardy gave in. "You're right. I can spare a few more bucks, at least enough to keep you in here for another few days."

Hardy pulled out a fifty and stuffed it in Doolittle's breast pocket.

"Don't let me down, buddy," Hardy said.

*   *   *   *

In his father's attic, Hardy removed the reichsmarks from the footlocker and stacked the 90 bundles in a pyramid. He shot several clear Polaroids of the money. Downstairs in the den, in the drawer next to Jabo's leather recliner, he found an envelope and addressed it to Sterling Auction Co., 110 Daulphine St., New Orleans; inserted the prints, along with a letter, and dropped it at the post office on his way to the office.

Chapter 16

▼

Klaus Kluge inserted Wagner's *Ride of the Valkyries* into the CD player and touched a button. As the music filled his Munich apartment, he prepared his afternoon coffee, a routine he enjoyed each day before opening his mail. He dropped a sugar cube in the brew and swirled in a generous helping of real cream. He sat down in an easy chair by the window, pressed a Gouloasis between his lips and lit it with a Zippo he had taken off an American POW during the war. He inhaled deeply and savored the music as it built to a rousing crescendo. The Fuhrer's favorite.

His apartment, a brownstone on the Prinzregentenplatz was elegantly furnished with thick rugs, heavy wall mirrors and rare antiques. From his third-floor window, he could see church spires rising above the city. Ah, and what a magnificent city, so rich with history. Just down the street at No. 16 was where the Fuhrer's apartment had once been. Ah, so long ago, but yet, it was like yesterday.

He sipped from the wafer-thin china cup and contemplated the missing Fuhrer document. The possibilities of what happened to it were endless. Berchtesgaden had been crawling with Allied soldiers during the final days of war. Any one of them could have taken the document. Wolfgang, a mere child at the time, had had only a vague memory of what had occurred. Finding the document was an impossible task. Most likely, it no longer existed.

Klaus picked up his mail and went through it, discarding the junk into a brass wastebasket. The last item was a large, thick envelope, which he recognized immediately. It was a sales catalog from Sterling Auction in New Orleans. They specialized in World War II militaria. He ripped open the package and turned to the section on World War II German items. A photo depicting a new listing caught his attention immediately. He did a double take, almost dropping his cup. "Nine million in reichsmarks!" Klaus read the details: "Lot A101. A rare collection of reichsmarks. All bills in denominations of 1,000 and sequentially numbered. Excellent condition. Bids close midnight January 31."

*   *   *   *

Klaus stubbed out his cigarette, gulped his coffee and hurried down to the ground level Luft Travel Agency office. He marched directly to a safe and spun the combination. Missed. Jittery, he took a deep breath and started over. This time when he turned the handle the steel door swung open.

Klaus removed a thick envelope from the back of the safe. Inside the envelope was a list of numbers of at least some of the reichsmarks that had been removed from the bunker in 1945.

Upstairs in his apartment, he unfolded the papers and placed them on the desk before him. He looked at his watch. 3:58 p.m. It would be 8:58 a.m. in New Orleans. The auction house probably opened at 9. He snatched up the phone and punched in the number of Sterling Auction, and waited. He lit another Gouloasis. Silently he counted the rings—two, three, four. He cursed.

"Good morning. Sterling Auction. May I help you?" It was a young woman's voice, soft and seductive.

"Good morning," Klaus said in his best English. "I just received your most recent catalog and I'm intrigued by the reichsmarks listing."

"Yes. We've had several inquiries already."

"The ad says that all of the bills are sequentially numbered. Is that correct?" Klaus asked.

"I think so. If you know the lot number, I'll pull it up on the screen."

Klaus read her the number and waited as computer keys clacked.

"Yes sir. They are numbered sequentially."

"I know you must be very busy, and I apologize," Klaus said, "but could you read me the number on the first bill?"

"No problem, sir." She read off a long serial number, which Klaus wrote down.

"Now, would you tell me the number on the last bill in the series?"

The young woman read it off, Klaus wrote it down. "Would you mind telling me who the vendor is?"

"I'm sorry, sir. I'm not allowed to give out that information. It's against company policy. I guess they figure potential buyers might contact the seller directly."

"Yes, I understand," Klaus said. "*Danke*." He hung up.

Klaus compared the two numbers given him with the first and last numbers on the list on his desk. A match.

＊　　＊　　＊　　＊

Hermann Blucker was relaxing at a table in the weinstube of the Shilthorn Hotel in Interlaken, enjoying a stein of Rugenbraun. Heinz Quackernack, his bodyguard approached.

"Herr Blucker."

"*Ja*." Blucker looked up through bushy brows, his black eyes shining like ebony behind the nickel-rimmed glasses.

"*Das Telefon*."

"Can't you see I'm enjoying my *bier*?" he snapped.

"It's Klaus, Herr Blucker. He says it's very important."

Blucker pushed away from the table. He hobbled on his cane to the phone in his private office, just off the lobby.

"*Hallo*?"

"Herr Blucker, some of the reichsmarks have surfaced."

"*Was sagten Sie*?"

"The reichsmarks have surfaced."

"Are you sure?" Blucker asked in a hushed tone.

"*Ja*."

"Where?"

"New Orleans."

"Who has them?"

"Sterling Auction Company."

"Who is offering them for sale?"

"I don't know."

"Find out!"

"*Ja*."

"And Klaus?"

"*Ja*, Herr Blucker?"

"Do not fail. The future of the Fatherland hangs in the balance."

* * * *

It was just past 8 p.m. and spitting snow when Ben Wasserman arrived home at his upscale Georgetown apartment. He dropped his leather briefcase on the couch and removed his coat and scarf. As usual, he had brought work home from the office. But first things first. He fed his gray tabby cat, and brought in a bundle of wood he had purchased at the supermarket and made a fire. While flames licked the logs, he pulled on sweats and slipped into a pair of well-worn leather house shoes. He poured three fingers of Glenlivet, found his reading glasses and retired to the couch, warmed by the fire and the scotch.

Unsnapping his briefcase, he removed a catalog from Sterling Auction Company. Ben made it his business to keep current with who sold German militaria, especially Nazi paraphernalia. One never knew what might turn up on the market. In the past, OSI had located and successfully prosecuted one Nazi war criminal after he tried to sell an exquisitely engraved SS dagger—his own. He sipped scotch and slowly turned the pages of the catalog. An unusual listing, one accompanied by a photograph of money stacked in a pyramid, caught his attention. "Nine Million in Reichsmarks! He read the details. The reichsmarks were in denominations of one thousand and sequentially numbered. Certainly worth looking into. He folded down the corner of the catalog page.

Chapter 17

Sarah called at a quarter of nine. "Hardy, I'm sick as a dog. Must be a virus." She sounded weak. "I'm not coming in today."

"No problem, I'll cover for you."

"Sylvia Birch, one of my divorce clients, has an appointment at two. Can you see her?"

"Sure. Anything I need to know about her case?"

"She suspects her husband is screwing around. I advised her she needed hard evidence. She may be ready to proceed, I don't know. Oh, I checked on a tag number she left with me. The name's in the file."

"I'll handle it. What else?"

"I can't think of anything," Sarah said. "I need to be working, but I feel terrible. I haven't even put up a Christmas tree."

"How about if I pick one up for you?"

"Would you? That's so thoughtful, Hardy."

"No problem. Now, you rest and don't worry about anything."

* * * *

Hardy had just signed a negligence complaint and handed it to Tommye Ann, when the front door opened, followed by the click of high heels. A tall woman stepped inside. It was the swing in her movement that caught his attention. She was wearing dark glasses, a belted beige trench coat, and tied around her head was a brown silk scarf.

"I hope I'm not late," she said, removing her shades and scarf. She finger-brushed her blonde hair. "I'm Sylvia Birch and I have an appointment with Ms. Dunnavant at two."

Tommye Ann explained that Sarah was ill. Hardy could only stare. She was fine. Nice cheek bones, wide mouth, full lips and stunning blue eyes. He stepped forward and smiled.

"Hi, I'm Hardy Jackson, Sarah's partner. She asked me to pinch hit for her today. May I take your coat?"

She stiffened and looked at him suspiciously for a moment, then said, "Yes, thank you."

Hardy hung her coat on a hall tree near the door. He found her file and escorted her back to his office, showing her a seat. "I had expected to see Ms. Dunnavant," she said coolly. "She's familiar with my case."

"She is awfully ill and didn't want you to make a wasted trip."

Sylvia crossed her legs and sat stiffly in her chair.

Hardy knew the first thing he had to do was gain her confidence. "Ms. Birch, I've handled numerous divorce cases, although I've never been through a divorce, I know it must be a traumatic experience."

"Yes, it is."

"And I know you must be hurting and perhaps confused about your legal rights.

"Yes."

She appeared to relax a notch.

"May I get you something to drink? Coffee perhaps?"

"No, thank you." She leaned forward in her chair and said in a low, measured tone. "Someone is bugging our phone!"

"How do you know?"

"I found the recording device in our attic."

"Any idea who?"

"I don't know. It could be my husband doing it, or maybe, someone is bugging him. I'm getting paranoid. That's the reason I'm running around dressed like Mata Hari."

"It's probably your husband," Hardy said. "Does he suspect that you're seeing someone?"

"I've given him no reason."

"Maybe he knows you're aware of his affair and he's trying to get some insurance, so to speak," Hardy said.

"I'm not doing anything!"

"He may now know that."

She told Hardy about finding Rudy's lipstick-smeared silk shorts. "I sealed them in a sandwich bag and hid them. If necessary, later on, I'll have them analyzed."

Hardy could barely suppress a smile thinking about labeling a man's dirty underwear as an exhibit and sticking them under the Warthog's nose. She'd probably have to excuse herself from the bench.

He remembered the note Sarah had placed in the file and got it out.

"The car is registered to Claudette Moreau. It says here that she's a French exchange student. Does that name mean anything to you?"

Sylvia searched her memory, her blues eyes narrowing. "No."

"It seems clear that your husband is carrying on an affair. What more do you want?"

"I know I can't go on living like this. But I'm afraid."

"Don't worry," Hardy said. "When you broadside him with a lawsuit he'll fold like wilted lettuce and settle the case."

"I-I don't know."

"Trust me, he will. All of them do."

"What happens when you file?"

"He'll have thirty days to hire a lawyer and answer in court. At the same time I file the complaint, I'll attach interrogatories—questions he must answer under oath—and request production of his financial records. He'll have forty-five days to produce his records. Then we'll set a date for his deposition. That'll put pressure on him to settle. Believe me, no man wants a woman poking around in his bank accounts."

"If you think so."

"There's nothing to worry about. Leave it to me."

"Should I remain in the house?" she asked.

"If you prefer."

"I had rather move out, but someone told me that would be abandonment."

"Nothing of the sort," Hardy said. "When people can't live together in peace, then someone has to move."

"If you think it won't harm my case, then I'll move out."

"Where do we serve papers on your husband?"

"He's in Austria. He should return within the week and most likely can be found at WorldWide Travel Agency."

Hardy asked if she had a photo of her husband. "One never knows in this business when someone will walk in and blow you away. It happens. At least I'll know who I'm dealing with."

She pulled a color snapshot from her billfold and handed it across the desk. Hardy studied the face. Penetrating eyes, thinning blonde hair combed straight back, oval face and a prominent nose. Hardy handed the photo back to the woman.

"I look forward to working with you, Ms. Birch. Believe me, this won't be as dreadful as you may think."

*   *   *   *

After Sylvia Birch departed, Hardy dictated a complaint for divorce. He alleged adultery, reserving the right to name the other party at a later date. This was a live grenade. Alleging the grounds in this manner usually scared the daylights out of the defendant, bringing out his worst paranoia. Keep 'em guessing. In the prayer for relief, he asked for equitable division of personalty and realty, alimony and attorney fees.

After Tommye Anne had transcribed the tape and printed out interrogatories and request for production of financial records, which he attached to the complaint, he carried the documents to the courthouse for filing.

It wasn't quite 4 p.m., but daylight was already fading. A cold wind blew. Hardy pulled his overcoat around him and trudged up the sidewalk toward the courthouse. Downtown was filling up with cars and people and he remembered it was the evening for the annual Christmas parade. He picked up his pace and climbed the brick steps of the courthouse two at a time.

The clerk's office was located on the second floor midway down a marble corridor. The clerk's door was open and Hardy walked in and laid the papers on the long wooden counter. Lewis Herman, the court clerk, had lost his right arm just below the elbow in a cotton gin accident many years ago.

"Hi'dy Hardy. How you today? Mighty sorry to hear about 'ye daddy pass'n. Can I help ya?"

"Thanks. I need to file these."

Herman held the documents fast to the counter with his stump and stamped a filing date with his left hand.

"See if you can manage to get these served on Christmas Eve," Hardy said.

Herman looked up, brows raised. "Must be a real special case."

Chapter 18

▼

At New Orleans Moisant International, Klaus ducked outside for a quick smoke, then got his luggage, purchased a city map, and hit the nearest bar. He downed a beer while locating Daulphine Street on the map. Daulphine was parallel to Bourbon in the French Quarter.

Afterwards, he hailed a Yellow Cab and settled into the back seat. Loud rap music blared from the radio. The cabbie turned down the volume and glanced at Klaus in the rear view mirror and said, "Where to, Mistah?"

Klaus pulled a scrap of paper from his shirt pocket and rechecked the address of Sterling Auction Company.

"One ten Daulphine Street."

The taxi jerked forward and was soon on the interstate rumbling east toward New Orleans.

It was humid. Klaus shed his coat.

On Daulphine Street, the taxi stopped in front of a two-story brick building with lacy wrought-iron grillwork around the second-story gallery. A sign with an arrow pointed upstairs to Sterling Auction Company.

"Vait for me." Klaus flashed two twenties at the cabbie. "I'll only be a minute."

Klaus exited the taxi, pulled open the iron grill door and climbed a winding stairwell to the second floor gallery. Sterling Auction was the third door on the left. It overlooked a brick courtyard surrounded by sculpted shrubs with a bubbling water fountain in the center. A sign on the office door gave business hours from 9-5. Klaus checked his watch. Almost closing time. He pushed open the heavy wooden door and entered the room. He saw no one. A black ceiling fan turned slowly. Shiny nail heads gleamed on the plank floor and plaster peeled from the walls. The place was old and seedy. A young woman, pretty, with long black hair, emerged from a back room, her purse and raincoat draped over one arm. Seeing Klaus unexpectedly, she stopped and stared at his black eye patch and scar.

"May I help you?" she asked.

"I apologize for coming in at this late hour," Klaus said, "but I've traveled a great distance to see the reichsmark collection your company is selling."

"We don't have them here. The vendor sent us a photo."

"Oh, I see! Perhaps you can tell me ver I can contact the owner."

"Sorry, that's against company policy." The woman walked over powered down a computer. "Now, if you will excuse me, I have to lock up for the day."

"Yes, of course." Klaus reached in his pocket and extracted a thick fold of bills fastened with a gold clip. He peeled off a hundred.

"Sir, please leave!" She pointed to the door, flicked off the lights and ushered Klaus out. Outside, after locking the door, she turned around and whispered to Klaus. "Meet me at the Cafe Desire in fifteen minutes. It's on Bourbon."

At the Desire, Klaus found a marble-top table by the window with a good view of the street and ordered a Dixie beer. The humidity was heavy enough to slice and the air was thick with the scent of fish. A black waiter, clad in a starched white smock placed freshly baked French bread on the table. "The boiled crawfish is mighty good, suh. Would you like a platter?"

"Perhaps later," Klaus said.

Klaus lit a Gouloasis, sipped his beer from a sweating mug and gazed out the window through a fine mist. The littered street was crowded with revelers drinking beer from paper cups. Dixieland jazz spilled into the twilight. Klaus caught a glimpse of something red. It was the young brunette. Tottering on spike heels, she picked her way around the puddles. Her slightly pigeon-toed gait pushed her backside out saucily to strain the fabric of her skirt. He felt a slight tightening in his groin and smiled smugly that a woman could still evoke such a response at his age. She entered the café with raincoat open and paused. Klaus raised his arm.

He stood as she approached and pulled out a chair. She sat and crossed her legs.

"Thank you," she said with a smile.

Klaus took his seat and inhaled her sweet scent. "How about something to drink?"

"Chardonnay will be fine." She searched Klaus's face with her large dark eyes.

"You are the man that called about the reichsmarks and asked about the serial numbers, aren't you?"

"My accent betrays me."

"Tell me. Why do you have such an interest in the reichsmarks?"

"I'm a collector."

"Of course. But I have to wonder why someone would travel from Europe to inquire about a catalog listing?"

"Sometimes the merchandise doesn't measure up to the advertisement. It's best to inspect before making an offer. Don't you agree?"

She ignored his question. "What's the name of the vendor worth to you?"

The waiter brought a glass of wine and set it on the table.

"At least a hundred dollars," Klaus said.

"Oh, I think it's worth much, much more to you."

Klaus' one blue eye glittered with a hardened amusement. "Do you have the information with you?"

"Yes. A thousand dollars and it's yours."

"Three hundred."

"Eight, and I'll forget I ever saw you." She pushed away from the table to leave.

"Just a minute." Klaus peeled off eight bills, folded and placed them on the table. The woman reached in her purse and withdrew a pack of Virginia Slims and a book of matches and slid the latter across the table to Kraus. She leaned toward him, a cigarette between her lips.

"Klaus opened the cover and tore out a match. Written on the inside cover was, "Joe Smith, PO Box 1100, Huntsville, Alabama." Klaus looked up at her with a lopsided smile. "My pleasure, *Fraulein*." He lit her cigarette. "You have made a very vise decision."

Chapter 19

Klaus drove a blue rented Chevy east toward a low, lumpy mountain. Just past the U.S. Space and Rocket Center, he stopped at a convenience store, purchased a city map and used the phone.

He drove slowly through a section of town littered with rundown houses, sleazy nightclubs and cheap motels, craning his neck to see the numbers on the buildings. He glanced at the map, then at a beige brick building down the street. U.S. Post Office. He turned into the parking lot and sat in the car for a moment studying the building. Glass enclosed a portion of the front. This offered a good view of people checking their boxes. He entered the building and surveyed the layout. Mailboxes were located to the right along two walls and at one end of the building. Number 1100 was about half-way down the inside wall—impossible to see from outside the building. That presented a problem. He returned to his car and sat for a long time, thinking. He didn't know what Joe Smith looked like. To find him, he would have to see the box being opened, but he couldn't stand around all day waiting for Smith to pick up his mail. Neither could he assume Smith would check his box every day.

He smoked. An idea came to him. What would happen if Mr. Joe Smith received a package too large for the post office box? A package that he would easily recognize when Smith carried it from the post office. Klaus drove to Wal-Mart, where he purchased binoculars, red wrapping paper and a cheap pair of tennis shoes. Checking into a nearby motel, he tossed the sneakers into the trash, stuffed the shoebox with paper and wrapped it in red, then drove back to the post office and mailed it.

Next morning, he parked across the street from the post office where he had an unobstructed view. He nervously flipped past radio stations and finally snapped off the racket. The traffic inside the post office was heavy early, then slacked off. Near noon, he noticed an untidy old man wearing a toboggan limp across the street and enter the post office. The old man emerged carrying something. He caught a glimpse of red. He grabbed the binoculars. He had a package under his arm, away from his line of sight. He adjusted the focus on the binoculars. The man stopped in the parking lot and looked at the package and held it to his ear and shook it. *Ja!* He felt a rush, his heart pounding with glee. He sat back and smiled as the man limped across the street and entered a room next to the Dumpster at the Mayflower Motel.

In his motel room, Doolittle held the red package to his ear and shook it hard. No rattle, no slosh, no sound at all. He looked at the return address, an unfamiliar Huntsville street. Probably a gift from a woman, he thought and tossed the package on the couch and walked into the bathroom, lifted the lid off the back of the toilet and pulled out his last bottle of Red Dagger. Already half gone, and he was running low on money. From now until the first of the month, he'd have to make do with whatever he could get his hands on. He unscrewed the cap and drained the bottle. The wine was sweet and smooth and didn't have much kick. He tossed the empty bottle in the wastebasket and plugged a Hank Williams tape into s small boombox.

Klaus sat in the car a few minutes in front of Room 123. He pulled a pack of Gouloasis from his front pocket, shook one out and lit it, then dropped the pack back in his shirt pocket. He finished the cigarette, and not seeing anyone, climbed out of the car and went to the door and pressed his ear against it. From inside, came the maudlin strains of country music. He knocked. No response. He rapped louder.

"Just a minute," came a muffled voice.

Klaus took a quick look back. No one. The lock clicked and the door swung open to reveal a disheveled old man with bloodshot eyes, obviously intoxicated. Klaus recoiled from the foul odor. He quickly scanned the room. On the tattered couch was the red package.

"Are you Joe Smith?" Klaus asked, trying to conceal his accent.

"Who wants to know?"

"The package you just picked up at the post office has postage due. They sent me over to collect."

Klaus placed a foot on the threshold and with one swift push barged inside the room. Doolittle groped for the phone by the bed. But Klaus seized him by the shoulder and spun him around, shoving him hard. Doolittle reeled backward and landed hard on the floor. Klaus kicked shut the door. Doolittle rose up on his elbows, blinked and shook his head. Klaus leaned over and backhanded the old man across the mouth, drawing blood.

"You aren't Joe Smith. Who are you?"

"Doolittle Brummett, you son-of-a-bitch," he said slowly.

"Tell me who Joe Smith is or I vill break your filthy neck."

"Don't hurt me anymore. Please."

"Talk!"

"I met 'im 'cross the street at Shirley's."

"Why are you picking up his mail?"

"He asked me to."

"Ver does he live?"

"Don't know."

"You are lying!" Klaus smacked Doolittle across the face.

"Noooo, please don't," Doolittle begged. "I swear I'm telling the truth."

Klaus shoved Doolittle back on the couch and ripped open his soiled pants and yanked them to his ankles.

"Nooooo, please."

Klaus grabbed Doolittle's testicles, squeezed and twisted them like lemons.

"Ahhhhhgg!"

"Now tell me the truth, you filthy swine!"

"Okay, okay, don't hurt me again, please."

"That's better."

"What do you wanna know?"

Klaus was in Doolittle's face. "Ver are the reichsmarks?"

"Joe has 'im...I guess."

"And ver does Joe live?"

"Let me up and I'll show ya."

Klaus nodded. Doolittle pushed up from the couch, grasping at the ragged edges of his fly. A car door slammed and Klaus turned his head toward the door. A bony knee smashed into his groin.

"Ahhhhh." The old German bent double, grabbing his crotch with both hands, gasping. Doolittle lunged for the door. Cursing, Klaus stumbled after him. Just as Doolittle grasped the doorknob, Klaus seized the back of his shirt and spun him around. One blow to Doolittle's jaw sent him flying against the wall. Doolittle grabbed his chest with both hands and tried to speak as he slid to the floor, leaving a dark smear of blood down the wall. He didn't move.

"Don't pass out on me." Klaus seized Doolittle by his shirt and shook his limp form. He felt for a pulse, grabbed the package, wiped the door clean with a handkerchief, and left.

Chapter 20

▼

Hardy sat in the Jeep for a full minute in front of Room 123, trying to shake his uneasiness. He switched off the ignition and walked to the front door. Muffled strains of Hank filtered through the flimsy door. Doolittle was home.

He knocked and looked around as he waited. The place was a hog pen. He pounded on the door again, twisted the knob and the door gave way. He squinted as he entered the dim, foul-smelling room, almost tripping over something. Doolittle was sprawled grotesquely on the filthy carpet, sightless eyes flared wide. His head rested in a puddle of blackening blood.

"Jesus!" Hardy lunged back against the wall and his eyes darted wildly around the room.

After he gathered his wits, he closed the door and went to where Doolittle lay. Squatting, he lifted Doolittle's hand to feel for a pulse. Cold, stiff and waxy, like a bar of soap. Doolittle must have had too much to drink, either tripped or passed out, hitting his head. Unless. Oh God. He could have been hurt worse than he thought a few days ago when he fell against the dresser. Maybe a concussion. If he got dizzy and fell and hit in the same spot again, it could have killed him.

Spying the phone, Hardy walked over to call 911, then stopped. Wait. He needed to think this out. That's when he saw the flip-top cigarette box on the carpet. He bent over and carefully picked up the box. Gouloasis. What would old Doolittle be doing with German cigarettes? The back of his neck tingled. He had to get the hell out of here. But what if someone had seen him enter the room? The police would want to know why he hadn't reported finding the body. Shit fire! They could try to pin Doolittle's death on him. Had he touched anything?

The doorknob! He could call the police later. Hardy stuffed the German cigarettes in his coat pocket and wiped the doorknob clean. He cracked the door and peeked out. Seeing no one, he stepped outside, and draping the knob with his handkerchief, pulled the door shut behind him and hurried to the Jeep.

It took all of the self-control he could muster not to squeal out of the parking lot. When he reached I-565, he turned west and stomped the accelerator. The needle climbed to 75.

Across from the motel, slouched low in the front seat of the blue Chevy, Klaus Kluge watched Room 123. The Dumpster partially blocked his view, but it was the only place he could park. He had been waiting there over an hour when a green Jeep pulled into the parking lot and stopped. A big man got out and walked in the direction of Room 123, then disappeared behind the Dumpster Had he entered Room 123? He was certain he did. Finally, his patience had paid off. The man he had seen reappeared from behind the Dumpster, got into his vehicle and drove away. He turned the ignition.

* * * *

Hardy leaned close to the steering wheel. A feeling of unfinished business nagged at him. He tried to remember everything he'd done in the room from the time he entered until the time he left: turned the doorknob, walked in, almost tripped on a foot, looked down and saw Doolittle…jumped against the wall scared shitless. His heart skipped a beat. The wall. His fingerprints were on the damn wall. He had to turn around and go back and wipe the wall clean. He glanced in his rearview mirror and saw a blue car moving up fast. An uneasy feeling gnawed at him. He slowed to 65 and the blue car slowed. He accelerated to 80. The blue car picked up speed.

At the Greenbrier exit he stomped the gas pedal to the floor, careened up the ramp and sped north on an unlined, two-lane asphalt road. He glanced in the rearview mirror. The blue car was gaining. No doubt now. He was being followed. The blast of a train whistle shattered his thoughts. He looked to his left, saw nothing, then snapped to his right. A long freight was moving toward his front, perpendicular to the highway. "Fuck!" He stomped the accelerator to the floor.

In front of him, red lights flashed and bells clanged. The train was approaching the crossing fast.

He glanced to his right again, trying to measure the distance to the train. Could he make it? His heart hammered mercilessly and his palms were so sweaty he could barely hold the steering wheel. A few more yards. "Come on, come on," he pleaded with the engine. He hit the raised crossing and the jeep went airborne, the train whistle blasting in his ears, as the freight roared by in back of him.

He was still trembling as he lowered the garage door behind him. He sat for a long time under the wheel, breathing deeply. Was the person in the blue Chevy a cop? Not likely. Cops radio other cops for assistance. He pulled the German cigarette box from his pocket and knew Doolittle's death had to be connected to the reichsmarks. Whoever was driving the blue Chevy would be looking for a green Jeep. He'd have to start driving Millie's Thunderbird.

Chapter 21

Ben Wasserman was dog-tired. He had been scouring through stacks of Army documents since early morning. He sat back in his chair and removed his reading glasses, closed his eyes and massaged his lids. He had found nothing of value in the mountain of papers. He got up from his desk and looked up Pennsylvania Avenue toward the Capitol. A slow rain was falling, turning the snow into mush. Why did the AG consider it so damned important that this individual be located? It would help if someone would clue him in. He sighed and stroked his hair. He reviewed the facts: Of the 127 rocket scientists that Von Braun had assembled in Bavaria in 1945, seven had children. Jacob had given him a list of their names. There was only one male child between the ages of eight and nine. And he was dead, killed in Vietnam in 1966.

Maybe he had been coming at this from the wrong direction. If he had been one of the German scientists trying to sneak a child into the U.S., how would he have done it? Certainly anyone smart enough to send a man to the moon could figure out a way to sneak a kid into this country.

Ben stroked his forehead. Perhaps he needed to back away from the problem. Take a break, go to a movie, get his mind off it and let his subconscious work on the problem for a while. Something clicked in Ben's brain. "Yes! Of course."

He went to the desk and plowed through the stack of files and documents until he found the list of female children between the ages of eight and nine who had accompanied their parents to America. He circled their names. There were three: Heidi Junge, Sonja Huber and Gretl Brandt. If they were alive today, they would be 55 or 56 years old. He buzzed Roberta. "Roberta, get Fletcher Preston, FBI supervisor in Huntsville, Alabama, on the line please."

"Yes, sir."

Ben leaned back in his swivel chair, chin resting on pyramided hands, staring at the phone. And waited.

The intercom buzzed. Ben jerked up the receiver. "Yes."

"Mr. Preston is on the line."

"Thanks." Ben punched the blinking button. "Fletcher, how are things down in Huntsville?"

"Everything moves re-al slow down he'ar, except the women."

"Working on anything interesting?" Ben asked.

"Yessuh. I can't talk about it, of course, but keep your eye on the newspaper. When this one pops, it'll make the evening news."

"I will." Ben cleared his throat, then turned serious. "Fletcher, I need your help."

"Name it. You know I'll do it if I can."

"Three female children, ages eight and nine years old, arrived in Huntsville in 1950 with their parents who were members of the German rocket team. I need photos and addresses."

"What are you OSI boys up to now?" Fletcher asked.

"Oh, you know. Just out chasing one thing and another."

"Still dogging Nazi's, huh? Most of them are dead or in nursing homes. Don't tell me our government is now going after their chill'n."

"Cute, Fletcher."

"Is this an official request?"

"I would rather keep paperwork to a minimum."

"Gotcha. You want me to go poking around asking questions about people who are good citizens down he'ar? There is a large, well-respected German community in Huntsville."

"Just a few discreet inquiries. Nothing more," Ben said.

"Give me the names and I'll see what I can do."

"I appreciate your help. I'm getting a lot of heat from upstairs so I would be doubly appreciative if you wouldn't let any kudzu grow under your ass."

"I'll see what I can do."

* * * *

"Good afternoon, Sterling Auction, may I help you?" It was a young woman's voice, soft and sexy.

"May I speak to the owner?" Ben said.

"He is away. I manage the office in his absence."

"My name is Ben Wasserman and I'm with the Office of Special Investigations, United States Department of Justice in Washington. Do you have a moment to answer a few questions?"

Ben heard her sharp intake of breath, then a moment of silence.

"What's this all about?" The sultriness had disappeared from the woman's tone, replaced by fear.

"Our office is interested in learning the identity of the vendor of the reichsmarks listed in your most recent catalog."

"We haven't violated any laws have we?"

"Nothing like that."

"Sir, I'm not supposed to release that information."

"We can do it the easy way or the hard way. Shall I request an FBI agent to visit you?"

"No. No, that won't be necessary. Just a minute." Computer keys clacked. "The name is Joe Smith."

"His address, please," Ben said, pen poised over pad.

"P.O. Box 1100, Huntsville, Alabama."

"Is that all the information you have on the vendor?"

"Yes, it is."

"Your government thanks you," Ben said.

He stared at the address on the pad. Huntsville. He grabbed for the phone and called Fletcher Preston, but couldn't reach him.

* * * *

There was a tap on his door.

"Enter."

An FBI courier stepped inside Ben's office. "Are you Ben Wasserman?"

"Yes."

"My instructions are to deliver this to you personally."

The courier handed Ben a sealed envelope with "Top Secret" stamped in black letters on the outside.

"Do you mind signing this receipt?" the man asked.

Ben whipped his signature onto the government form. He sliced through the thick paper and dumped the contents of the envelope onto his desk.

It was the information from Fletcher Preston typed on standard FBI forms. Each was accompanied by a photo of the subject and several news clippings.

Ben scanned through the report on Sonja Huber. Born Feb. 2, 1940, in Berlin to Dr. Eric and Gertrude Huber, she had come to the United States, arriving in Huntsville in 1947. She graduated from Huntsville High School in 1959, got her masters degree from the University of Alabama and presently taught high school in Huntsville. There was a page from her high school yearbook showing that she had been a member of the National Honor Society, Beta Club and a cheerleader.

Ben dug through the stack of Army files on his desk, found Dr. Eric Huber's, then compared his current information with the file, for inconsistencies. The Army files verified that Huber had a daughter named Sonja. He laid the Huber file aside and picked up the file on Heidi Junge. It didn't offer much help either. She was married to a neurosurgeon in Mobile, and according to news clippings, seemed to spend most of her time doing charitable work. Again, Ben compared his current information on the woman with information in the Army file. He found no inconsistencies.

The report on Gretl Brandt was the briefest. She had drowned in 1948 at the age of eight in Lake Konigssee near Berchtesgaden. The family had returned to Germany to visit relatives, and while on a picnic, the child had fallen out of a boat and drowned. Her body was never found. Afterwards, the parents, Dr. Helmut and Eva Brandt, had adopted a boy in Germany, the child of a family member killed during the Battle of Berlin. Dr. and Mrs. Brandt were dead.

Ben looked at the small black and white photo of Gretl that was stapled to the 1945 Army interrogation report. She wore dark, horn-rimmed glasses and looked very brainy. Her long hair was braided in the fashion of that day. He read her physical characteristics on the report—weight, height, complexion. She had brown eyes and brown hair. Then he cross-checked this information against that of her parents. According to the 1945 Army report, both parents had blue eyes.

Ben drummed the desktop with his fingers and waited for Fletcher Preston to answer his phone. He hated calling his home, especially on Sunday afternoon. Six rings. Maybe Preston was on the links or had gone to see a movie.

"Hello," purred a female voice. Music played in the background.

"I was trying to reach Fletcher Preston," Ben said not sure he had called the correct number.

"He's in the shower. Can you hold?"

"Sure."

Ben was quite certain that he had interrupted a romantic interlude.

"Preston." The voice was brusque.

"Fletcher, Ben Wasserman here. I apologize for disturbing you at home, but I wanted to thank you for sending the information I requested."

"Glad to assist. But I have a feeling you didn't call just to thank me."

"You're right. There is one more favor I need to ask of you."

"Right."

"Recently a Joe Smith rented a post office box in Huntsville. I would like a background check on this man. Do you think you could help me?"

"I'll see what I can do? What's the box number?"

"Eleven hundred. It's the West Huntsville Station."

"Got it," Preston said.

"And Fletcher, do have a pleasant afternoon."

Chapter 22

▼

Hardy sat motionless at his desk, his eyes fixed on a knot in the walnut paneling. He didn't know what to do about reporting Doolittle's death. Should he call the police and tell them what he knew? If he did, it could lead the killer straight to him—if there was a killer. Whichever way he turned there was danger. Be arrested for murder, or be murdered. He had been checking the newspaper daily and watching the news. The only mention of Doolittle was a death announcement in the paper. He figured it was only a matter of time before the cops lifted his prints from the motel room, sent them to the FBI Crime Lab and matched them up.

What scared the BeJesus out of him was not the thought of cops slapping cuffs on him, but some German lurking around with God knows what on his mind. He trembled at the thought.

If only he had someone to talk to, share his burden, give him direction. Millie, once his rock, mustn't know. Keeping everything penned up was tearing his guts apart.

* * * *

Sarah's black Volvo was parked in front of her apartment at the Royal Foxes, an upscale complex east of town. It was cold and the sky gray. No one stirred, except one idiot jogger huffing down the street, trying to add a millisecond to his life.

He parked the Thunderbird and hurried up the metal stairs to Sarah's apartment. When he reached the landing, he put an ear to the door. The low rumple of a TV came from inside. His heart was doing somersaults. He knocked, timidly at first, then harder the second time. There was a scraping noise inside. That would be Jasmine pushing her stool up to the peephole.

"It's Mister Hardy, mommy," she yelled.

The security chain rattled, a lock thumped and the door swung open. Jasmine, wearing red Santa Claus pajamas, was standing just inside the door. Cartoons blared from the TV. He knelt down and handed her a piece of chewing gum.

"Hi, sweetheart, how are you?"

"Mommy says gum causes cavities."

"Here, take it."

"Hardy!"

"Give me a break, Sarah."

Sarah studied his ashen face for several seconds. "You look like you just met death. What's wrong?"

"Plenty. I'm in deep shi—" he looked around at Jasmine. "Deep trouble."

Sarah shot a stern look at Jasmine and ordered, "Stay in here and watch cartoons. Mister Hardy and I will be in the kitchen."

"Can I have the gum, mommy?"

Sarah frowned. "I guess so. But just this once."

Sarah showed Hardy to a glass-top table in the kitchen, retrieved two brown mugs from the cabinet and filled them with coffee. She set one mug in front of Hardy and sat down with the other across the table from him.

"Hardy, have we been sued for malpractice?"

"No—no. Nothing like that."

She exhaled loudly. "Thank God."

"I don't know where to begin," Hardy said.

Sarah sipped her coffee, studying Hardy over the rim of her cup, listening.

He began with Jabo's death. "'Leave it be', he said. Over and over. I had no idea what he was talking about. Now, I think he was trying to warn me off the footlocker. While doing the estate inventory, I sawed the lock off the footlocker and found nine million reichsmarks."

Sarah's eyes widened. "You can't be serious!"

"Oh, yes. Unfortunately, the reichsmarks were nearly worthless by the end of the war, and after the war they were exchanged for deutschemarks. The only value they have now are as collectibles."

Sarah frowned. "I thought you were going to tell me you were suddenly a millionaire."

He told her about listing the reichsmarks with Sterling Auction in New Orleans and how he had obtained a post office box in Huntsville under an assumed name.

"Hardy, are you sure you're not trying out a new plot in one of your novels?"

"I wish to God I were."

"Then what happened?"

"After I rented the box, I met an old drunk named Doolittle who lived in a flea bag motel nearby and persuaded him to pick up my mail. When I stopped by his room to get my mail, I found him dead!"

"Murdered?"

"I don't know." He described the blood under Doolittle's head, "I suppose he could have been drunk and fallen, except for what I found in his room—a box of German cigarettes."

"Maybe they were Doolittle's."

"No, he smoked Lucky's. But that isn't all. When I saw the cigarettes, I knew something was wrong. I hightailed it from the room, jumped in my Jeep and hauled ass. I was scared shitless."

"Don't tell me you're a murder suspect."

"Not yet, anyway. But someone saw me leave the motel."

"Are you sure?"

"They chased me all the way to Greenbrier." He told her about beating the freight train and escaping.

"Who…?"

"My guess it was Doolittle's killer."

Sarah turned pale and her brown eyes bore into his. "Then whoever killed Doolittle is looking for you?"

"That's the way I figure it."

"God, Hardy, this is what's been eating you lately at the office. I'm sorry for giving you so much grief about it."

"I have really stepped in something this time, Sarah."

"What have the police recommended?"

"I haven't contacted them. I'm afraid if I do, they'll lead the killer straight to me."

"Hardy, this is serious business. You could be charged, if not with murder, then with obstructing justice."

"I'll take my chances. I'd rather be arrested than murdered."

"What is all this about?" she asked. "Why would anyone care about worthless German money?"

Hardy gazed out the kitchen window and chewed his lip.

"I wish to God I knew."

"There has to be something else. What else was in the locker?"

He stared into his coffee cup for several moments. "Yes. There was something else."

"What?"

"A paper of some kind. It was an envelope with a document inside."

"What did it say?"

"I don't know. I couldn't read it. It was written in German."

"Where is it? Maybe I can translate it."

Hardy's eyes narrowed. "What did I do with it?" A pause. "I put it in the pocket of my windbreaker. I had forgotten about that."

"Where is it?"

"Home."

* * * *

Millie was asleep on the den couch. Aubie was curled up at her feet. An old Humphrey Bogart movie was on TV.

Hardy tiptoed over and kissed her on the forehead, then went to the bedroom and found the windbreaker and the document in the pocket.

Chapter 23

▼

Rudy was back home from Austria and with a stomach bug. A slow, cold drizzle fell. He parked his green BMW in a south Huntsville strip mall near WorldWide Travel and dashed inside, checked his messages, then departed for home.

He sloshed back through the rain to his car and opened the door.

"Sir, are you Rudolph Birch?"

Startled, Rudy whirled around. A deputy sheriff was towering over him.

"You're a hard man to find," the deputy drawled. "I have some papers for you, sir." He thrust a thick sheaf of folded documents into Rudy's hand.

Rudy stood in the drizzle watching dumfounded as the deputy squeezed into a brown and white cruiser and drove off.

Inside the BMW, he unfolded the papers and saw a summons stapled to the front. A lawsuit! He swallowed hard and flipped back the summons to scan the first page. A divorce action. And she wanted alimony.

"Gold-digging bitch," he said through clenched teeth. He closed his eyes and took several deep and slow breaths and attempted to relax. She had accused him of adultery and, in addition to alimony, wanted half of everything he owned, plus attorney fees. But that wasn't all. Stapled to the back of the lawsuit were another fifty pages of interrogatories and a request for all of his financial records.

What a fucking nightmare. The worst thing that could possibly happen to him—especially at this time. It must not happen. It wasn't going to happen. He cursed Sylvia and drove home.

The house was quiet as a tomb. No Sylvia. He found Imodium in the bathroom and took a slug to settle his stomach. Afterwards, he showered and slipped into his robe. It was then that he found a scrawled note on the breakfast bar propped between the salt and pepper shakers.

> Rudy, sorry to spoil your Christmas, but you destroyed my world with your screwing around. I thought it best that I move out. See you in court.
>
> Sylvia.
>
> P.S. Bon jour to Claudette—or is it *bon appetit*?

He crushed the note in a fist and banged the bar. "Damn her to hell!" The bitch was fucking up everything.

Anger would solve nothing. He had to think matters out carefully. And see a good lawyer.

He was sick and ought to be in bed. He slipped into an expensive cashmere jacket, grabbed his belted trench coat and was out the door in 10 minutes.

*   *   *   *

At the Pen South Tower, a modern glass and brownstone, he turned in and parked in the multi-level garage.

In the lobby, he studied the directory for a moment, then stepped into the polished brass elevator and punched the tenth floor button. The doors slid back and he stood facing double wooden doors with ornate gold-plated handles.

Rudy pulled open the door and stepped into a cave of deep pile green carpeting and subdued lighting. A young blonde with a lot of teeth looked up from behind her desk with a perky "Good afternoon sir. May I help you?"

Rudy coughed nervously. "Yes, is Mr. Buttner in?"

"And your name, sir?"

"Tell him Rudolph Birch is here and that I need to see him immediately."

"Do you have an appointment, sir?"

"No, I was hoping he could work me in. It's very important."

"Please have a seat and I'll see if he's in."

Rudy eased into a brown leather chair and reached for a magazine. He checked his watch. His palms were moist and his heart pounded. He was feverish.

God, he hated this. He tossed the magazine aside and picked up another and tried to read an article, but his mind wouldn't cooperate.

"Hello, Rudy. How are you?" Buttner, lean and tanned, strode in buttoning a double-breasted, gray pinstriped suit. Rudy rose to his feet.

"I'm not very well, I'm afraid," Rudy said, shaking the younger man's hand. "I don't know if you remember me, but we played a threesome in a benefit tournament last summer."

"Of course, I remember. And how's the travel business?"

"Good."

Buttner chatted amicably as they walked down to his office.

"Please, be comfortable." Buttner pointed to a chair. "May I get you something to drink?"

"No, thanks. I'll get right to the point." Rudy leaned forward in his chair. "I hardly know where to begin. My wife has filed for divorce"

"I see," Buttner said with a studied frown.

"I went to Austria and when I returned, I was served these." Rudy pushed the papers across the desk to Buttner who glanced quickly through them.

"I need a good divorce lawyer and I hear you are the best in Huntsville."

Buttner's face brightened. "That's probably overstated."

"Will you represent me?"

"Certainly. My retainer is twenty-five thousand. That's up front."

"That seems high."

"Yes, I agree," Buttner said.

"I can pay the fee. That's no problem."

"Fine." Buttner placed a clean yellow pad in front of him and uncapped a pen. "Now, let's get down to business. When were you served the summons and complaint?"

"This morning."

"Excellent. That gives us plenty of time to prepare an answer. We have thirty days to respond."

"I don't mind the divorce, and wouldn't be adverse to giving her some alimony," Rudy said. "But she wants to see all of my financial records. Can she do that?"

"Within limits."

"That can't happen."

Buttner put on reading glasses and carefully perused the complaint, nodding occasionally. "I see it was filed in French Springs by Hardy Jackson."

"Do you know him?"

"Unfortunately, yes. Mostly from my service on the Grievance Committee."

"Is he good?"

"He's an ambulance chaser. I assure you he is not someone to fear—especially in a divorce action."

"That's good news." Rudy relaxed somewhat. "As I said, I'm not opposed to a divorce. But I am greatly concerned about the request for all of my financial records. Can you prevent this from happening?"

"I'm afraid not. Each party has a right to full and complete discovery of all assets acquired during the marriage."

"My God, this can't be happening!"

"Your wife is entitled to ask for an equitable division of assets and the court must know what they are," Buttner said.

"We've got to trip her up or at least slow her down."

"That, I can do," Buttner said. "First, I will file a motion alleging improper venue and ask the Court to transfer the case to Huntsville. That will give us some extra time."

"Can you file a motion to dismiss this nonsense?" Rudy said. "What if I take the position I don't want a divorce?"

"That doesn't apply to divorce cases. Condonation is a defense, but it's seldom asserted anymore."

"Explain that, please."

"The complaining party—your wife in this instance—condones what you did. For example, if you and she resume a normal marital relationship and carry on sexual relations you're entitled to plead condonation."

"Buy me all the time you can."

Chapter 24

▼

Special Agents Fletcher Preston and Hank Duckworth sat in an unmarked gray, Chevy parked on a Huntsville side street where they had been waiting for more than an hour. It was almost dark and very cold.

Duckworth, sitting behind the wheel, zipped up his black FBI windbreaker and cupped his hands and blew on them. "You reckon she got wind of what's up?"

"She probably stopped for groceries."

Afternoon traffic was steady. The two men fell silent and concentrated on the vehicles whizzing up Governors Drive. Shortly, the two-way radio crackled.

"Subject is proceeding east up Governors in a pink Town Car."

Preston looked over at Duckworth behind the wheel. "Be ready."

Duckworth turned the ignition and eased the car in gear, keeping his foot on the brake.

"There she goes!" Preston pointed. Duckworth stomped the accelerator and the Chevy shot out onto Governors Drive. A pick-up truck barreling down the mountain swerved and braked, horn blowing, and barely missing them. The driver rolled down his window and shouted an obscenity.

"Damn, that was too close," Duckworth said.

"Keep your eye on the mark." Preston grabbed a portable blue light from the floorboard and slapped it on the dash. Duckworth gunned the Chevy and wove through traffic, gaining on the Town Car. The brake lights flashed on as it slowed for a traffic light.

"We're in luck." Preston said. "Block her!"

Duckworth swerved sharp right, out of the lane, roared up the road shoulder slinging gravel and skidded to a stop in front of the Town Car.

Preston jumped out of the Chevy and ran over and jerked open the door. Duckworth rammed the Chevy in park, scrambled out and ran to the passenger side, his hand resting on the butt of a holstered 9 mm SIG Sauer.

"Are you Magdalene Webber?" Preston barked.

The woman, her face a mixture of fear and confusion, could barely speak.

"Yes—yes I am."

Preston flashed his credentials in her face. "FBI, ma'am. Step out of the car."

He switched off the ignition. The woman's face was pale and her hands shook.

"What is this? I don't understand." Her voice was barely audible.

"Ma'am, you're under arrest. Please step out."

Sunny reached for her purse. Preston snatched it from her hand. Trembling, Sunny Webber climbed out of the car and stood unsteadily, holding to the door.

Preston read her rights, then cuffed her.

Duckworth radioed for a wrecker to tow her car. A mobile unit from a local TV station was already on the scene, lights glaring and camera rolling. Preston hustled Sunny over to the Chevy, held open the door and loaded her in the back.

"What am I being arrested for?" Sunny asked.

"Money laundering, drug trafficking, engaging in a criminal enterprise, just to name a few."

During the trip downtown Sunny was quiet, except for constantly clearing her throat. Duckworth swerved into the sally port beneath the courthouse and jerked to a stop near the elevator.

"I'm dying for a cigarette," Sunny said.

Preston twisted around in the front seat and looked at Sunny. "Sorry, ma'am. It's against the rules."

"Do you think I care about your damn rules?"

"Sorry."

"I have something to say you'll be interested in. And I want a cigarette before I say it."

Preston thought for a moment then, glanced over at Duckworth behind the wheel and made a gimme motion. Duckworth dug a pack of Marlboros from his pocket and handed it to Preston. Preston lit a cigarette and held it to Sunny's lips. She inhaled hard and deep and held the smoke in her lungs a long time with her eyes closed and exhaled slowly. "Thanks. What's the next stop?"

"Book you and then take you before a U.S. Magistrate in the morning."

"Another, please." She looked at the cigarette between Preston's fingers.

Preston held the cigarette to her lips and she took another long pull on it, blowing smoke from her nostrils and mouth simultaneously.

"Tell me about immunity for the exchange of testimony," she said.

"That's something you'll have to take up with the U.S. Attorney," Preston said.

"When he hears what I have to say, he'll be interested. Call him tonight."

* * * *

The phone rang. Ben answered.

"Wasserman." His voice was curt.

"Ben, this is Fletcher Preston."

"What's on you mind, Fletch?"

"Remember me telling you several weeks ago that we were onto something big down here?"

"I remember," Ben said.

"We made a major bust tonight. It looks like one of the largest cocaine operations in the Southeast. One of Huntsville's leading citizens was laundering the drug money through her real estate business."

"My congratulations to you on your success. But couldn't it have waited until morning?"

"The lady is ready to cut a deal. She wants to speak to someone in OSI."

"What does money laundering have to do with tracking down Nazis?" Ben asked.

"She wouldn't say much, but what little she did say, it's the wildest story I've ever heard."

"Give me a hint," Ben said.

"Does the disappearance of a boy that came here with the German rocket team mean anything to you?"

Ben shot from the couch. "What did she tell you?"

"That's about all I can say over the phone. She won't talk to anyone except the OSI."

"I'll be on the first flight out."

*   *   *   *

The county jail was located on the top floor of the courthouse where the air was stale and rife with body odor. Ben and Preston signed the register at the front desk.

The jailer, a portly white man with long, gray sideburns levered himself slowly out of the chair and picked up a large silver key ring. "Ya'll foller me."

They followed as he wobbled down a concrete corridor. At a gray, steel door he stopped and pulled it open.

"Ya'll make yo'selves at home," he said. "I'll have her sent down in a minute." He ambled off down the hallway.

Ben scraped back a wooden chair and sat down at a small table. The room was a steel box, not much larger than a walk-in closet. There were no windows. A narrow slit in the door, just large enough to accommodate a plate of food, was the only opening.

Down the hallway, Ben heard the clanging of steel, followed by the squeak of footsteps on concrete. The cell door creaked open and a matron ushered a white female prisoner into the room, followed by a middle-aged man with a ponytail. He wore an expensively cut blue suit and black cowboy boots.

"Holler when you're ready to leave," the matron said and departed.

The man spoke first. "Gentlemen, I'm Bobby Joe Carlton. I represent Ms. Webber." He shook hands, first with Preston then Ben. "Of course, you know my client." Preston nodded to Sunny.

Ben did the same and said. "I'm pleased to meet you."

Carlton pulled out a chair for Sunny and she sat down and placed her manicured hands on the table in front of her.

Carlton placed a tape recorder on the table and clicked it on. "Gentlemen, my client, after having been advised by me, is ready to talk with you. Please proceed."

Preston set his tape recorder in the middle of the table. After a preliminary statement including the date, time and the names of those present, he read Sunny her rights once more. "Ben Wasserman is with the Office of Special Investigations."

Ben cleared his throat and leaned forward in his chair.

"I understand you have information you think our office might be interested in."

Sunny looked up at her lawyer and wet her lips. "See if he has any credentials." Her voice was thin and raspy and filled with uncertainty.

"Yes, of course." Ben reached in his hip pocket and produced a plastic laminated document. They looked at the photo then at Ben, apparently satisfied.

"What I know will rock Washington," she said without batting an eye.

"That's quite a teaser."

"And Europe also," she added.

"I'm listening."

"My client wants assurances from the government, Mr. Wasserman," Carlton said.

"What kind of assurances?"

"Immunity from prosecution on all charges."

"I have no authority to grant immunity," Ben said. "That must come from the highest level in Justice."

"I also want written guarantees that I will be placed in the Witness Protection Program," Sunny said. "Once I talk, my life won't be worth two cents."

"Because of your alleged involvement in drug trafficking or the matters you feel I'm interested in?" Ben asked.

"Both."

Ben knew he had to be cautious. He couldn't get hasty. One procedural mistake and a solid case could go down the drain.

"I can't promise you anything," he said. "You must provide me with enough information to interest my superiors in Washington."

"Very well," said Sunny. "In 1946, a five-year-old boy was spirited into this country posing as the child of a rocket scientist. He wasn't."

Ben felt his heart bang against his chest. He almost smiled, but caught himself. The woman might provide a solid lead. "That is interesting," he said, studying Sunny's face and brown eyes, looking for some sign of deceit. "But we have hundreds of young children coming across our border each month."

"Not like this one," she said.

"Oh?"

"Does it interest you, Mr. Wasserman, why a German scientist would smuggle a child into this country?"

"Why don't you tell me?"

"If the boy was not the son of the couple who brought him here, then who was he? And why did they do this?"

"I don't know. Tell me."

"You're interested, then?"

"Definitely."

"Enough that you will talk to your superiors about immunity?"

"You haven't told me anything yet."

"I was born in Germany in 1941," she said. "My father, I'm told, was sent to the Eastern Front and never returned. My mother subsequently married an American serviceman after the war and we emigrated to Huntsville in 1949. Our family became acquainted in the German community. We all knew each other and frequently visited together. I played with their children and we spent the nights at each other's homes and attended parties together, that kind of thing. Children hear things. You know what I mean?"

Ben nodded.

"Sometimes they hear things they aren't supposed to hear. I was spending the night at a friend's house when I heard adults speaking German in low voices. At first I didn't know where the voices were coming from. Then I realized they were coming from an air vent near my bed. I could hear everything they were saying." Sunny paused and wet her lips. "What I heard didn't mean a lot to me at the time, but I knew it was a great secret by the way they spoke. They were whispering about a boy named Wolfgang, and when they spoke of him it was with great reverence. I knew that whoever Wolfgang was, he must be important."

"Do you know how they sneaked the boy into the country?" Ben asked.

"Yes. Disguised as a girl."

"How?"

"Somehow they brought him in disguised as a girl, then shortly afterwards they flew back to Germany to visit family and while there, the story goes, the girl drowned in Lake Konigsee, near Berchesgaden. Her body was never found. The parents brought back their young nephew whose family had been killed in the war."

"Let me guess," Ben said. "There was no drowning. The two children were one and the same."

"Correct."

Ben smiled. "Is Wolfgang still alive?"

"Very much."

"What name does he use today and where does he live?"

"When my lawyer has received a written guarantee of immunity and protection, then I will give you that information."

Chapter 25

▼

Sarah barged into Hardy's office. He was slumped in his wingback chair staring at the wall.

"Hardy, you can't spend the rest of your life sitting back here with the door closed."

"I'm scared. Just look at my hands." Hardy held both hands in front of him. They trembled. "I was okay for a while. Now, I'm crashing. Every time a new client comes in I wonder if it's Doolittle's killer coming for me. I don't know if the killer is a man or a woman, German or American. It could be anyone. Not knowing is the scary part. But, I've got protection. And you might want to do the same."

"What are you talking about?"

Hardy reached under a tented newspaper on his desk and lifted out a Smith & Wesson .44 magnum and pointed the barrel toward the ceiling. "If someone reaches to scratch his ass, I may waste him."

"Put that away, please! I can't stand the sight of those things."

He placed the revolver under the newspaper.

"You're being ridiculous and melodramatic," she said.

He handed Sarah a document, a single sheet of good quality bond. At the top was an eagle standing on a wreath encircling a Swastika. He watched Sarah's face and eyes as she silently read the document.

"What does it say?"

"S-h-h, just a minute." Her eyes grew wide and her face animated. "My God!"

"What?"

"I can't believe this."

"Tell me."

"This is incredible."

"What does it say?"

Sarah was speechless.

"Dammit! What does it say?"

"Do you realize what this is?" she whispered.

"Tell me!"

"It's signed by Adolf Hitler. Power of attorney from Hitler giving the bearer legal authority to access a bank account. In Switzerland."

Hardy's eyes danced as he tried to comprehend what he had just heard. He jerked the document from Sarah's hand. "You sure this is real?"

She pointed to the foot of the document. "Look, here's Hitler's signature with two witnesses and an attestation clause with a magistrate's seal."

Hardy examined Hitler's signature. It was a palsied scrawl, witnessed by Martin Bormann and Nicolaus von Bulow. He rubbed his finger across the raised seal. The document was typed and dated, Berlin, April 29, 1945.

"Where did your father get this document?"

"I don't know. I found it in his Army footlocker with the reichsmarks."

"You know what this means?" Sarah said, her eyes growing wider. Hardy met her gaze but didn't reply. "There may be millions, even billions of dollars stashed away in this bank account, and they will come looking for us." She swallowed. "If they haven't already."

Hardy was silent, deep in thought.

"Did you hear me, Hardy?"

"Yeah, I heard you." He turned and looked at Sarah. "Did you say the power of attorney was made to bearer?"

Sarah stared at Hardy with disbelief. "No way, Hardy!"

"Why not?" Think about it. We could be so rich we would never have to work again."

"Are you crazy? They would kill us if we tried to touch a penny of that money."

"What are we going to do with it?"

"Burn it," Sarah said.

Chapter 26

Millie's cancer and the wasting chemo, a mysterious German document, Doolittle's death, a car that may or may not have chased him back from Huntsville. That night his thoughts collided as each scrambled to take its place in some unfathomable hierarchy of reason.

Millie slumbered fitfully beside him, alternately shivering and clutching the covers under her chin only to swat them away minutes later. He had to get her out of here and find a place where he could think, too.

"Sarah, can you cover for me at least until the middle of next week?" said Hardy into the downstairs hall phone shortly after 8 a.m. the next day. "Nothing's coming up on the docket and the appointment book looks light. I'll have Tommye Ann reschedule my clients."

"Hardy? What's going on? I didn't close my eyes all night after I translated that damn document yesterday. And what did you do with it?"

"For now, you don't need to know where it is. I need to get away. Please, Sarah. Jabo's fishing buddies have a cabin up on White Lake in West Tennessee. I'm going to take Millie up there for a few days since the weather has warmed. The fresh air will do her good and maybe I can get this mess straightened out in my mind. You can reach me on my cell phone."

* * * *

The old cabin had not been used since last summer. After Millie unpacked and put away the few groceries they'd bought at the general store on the way up, the two of them had strolled the edge of the lake, their fingers linked, until dusk closed in and the chill drove them inside.

Hardy built a fire with twigs and fallen branches he'd picked up on their walk and they turned in early. He lay on his back staring at the moon-silvered rafters overhead, wondering if life would ever be simple and good again. The drive up earlier that day had been leisurely, and once they'd crossed the Tennessee line, he'd wanted nothing more than to just keep driving north.

A night creature skittered across the cedar shake roof and Millie moved closer to him, trailing her fingertips down the skin on the inside of his arm.

"I haven't been much of a wife to you these past few months," she murmured against his neck.

Hardy gathered her fragile body to him. "Don't worry about that for now, sweetheart. All I want is for you to get better. Shucks, darlin', you're a firecracker. I needed a break to cool down."

She chuckled softly and after a while the two slept entwined until dawn turned the far edge of the lake pink.

The days on White Lake passed much too quickly. And then it was time to head home. He knew what he had to do now. Just as Sarah said. Burn the damn document and pray Doolittle's death was an isolated event that had no connection with the document. Maybe the nightmare would just go away.

* * * *

It was after 10 p.m. when Klaus Kluge parked the blue Chevy down the block from the two-story white clapboard where Hardy Jackson lived. A cold, misty rain fell. Satisfied that no one was at home he got out and made his way up the sidewalk toward the house. At the back was a sliding glass door that opened onto a deck. Unless there was a broom handle inserted at the bottom of the sliding doors, it would be easy to get in. He pressed both palms against the glass and pushed up. The inside lock disengaged. Easy. Then he slid the door open. No broom handle. How trusting these stupid Americans are.

Inside, the house was dark except for a nightlight in the hallway. He clicked on a flashlight and strolled through the downstairs, pulling open drawers, searching cabinets and prowling through closets, looking for the document. No luck. It could be upstairs in one of the bedrooms. He slowly climbed the carpeted staircase to the second floor. When he reached the second floor landing, a low hissing sound came out of the darkness. He reached for the pistol inside his coat pocket, simultaneously pointing the flashlight toward the sound. Caught in the high beams was a gray cat, back bowed up in the shape of a horseshoe and hair standing on end. Klaus let out a sigh of relief and pocketed his pistol.

"You scared hell out of me."

He squatted down and turned the light away from the animal.

"Kitty, kitty, kitty," he extended his hand toward the cat.

*   *   *   *

Millie was dozing against the headrest when Hardy pulled onto Beauregard Street. It was the old section of town. Metal historic markers proclaiming construction date and past and current owners dotted well-manicured lawns. When he reached a marker that read "1905 Wilson-Jackson House," he killed the headlights and circled the block looking for unfamiliar cars. The yellow bulb under the carport glowed dimly in the twilight. Everything appeared normal. He circled the block once more and pulled up into the carport. Millie roused and rubbed her eyes.

"Let's go in and get you bedded down," said Hardy. "I'll come back out for our bags."

At the back door, Hardy reached around Millie, keys extended and opened the door. An overwhelming stench churned from the dark recesses of the house. Hardy yanked out his handkerchief and held it to his face. Millie made feeble retching sounds and he reached for her and drew her under his arm. Something was dead. Aubie? He glanced down at the plastic placemat on the floor just inside the door where Aubie's nearly full food and water dish sat.

"Stay here," he ordered Millie. "Better yet, get in the car and lock the doors until I come back for you."

Hardy glanced around, looking for Aubie. 'Kitty, kitty." He flipped the switch for the overhead kitchen light, but the power was out. He stumbled over cooking implements strewn about the floor and kicked them aside with an echoing clatter.

"Damn!" He made his way through the house following the ever-stronger odor. It was coming from the front of the house. He searched while clutching his handkerchief to his face. His eyes stung, saliva collected on his tongue and he swallowed repeatedly, but he searched on, desperate to zero in on the overpowering stench. He crept through the dark, making his way through the rooms on the ground floor—dining room, den and living room. The hulking silhouette of the baby grand sat in the alcove of the bay window, its black lacquer finish glowing in the filtered light of the street lamps. The clock chimed 7 near the front door. He went to the bay window and tugged up one of the side sashes to let some air into the dank room, turned and nearly fell over the piano bench. Cautiously, he lifted the piano lid and the nearly visible cloud of odor made him reel and he dropped the lid with a loud crash. He swallowed hard a couple of times. He steeled himself and lifted the lid once more. Poor Aubie. Swollen twice his size.

He went to the kitchen and jerked open the drawer where Millie kept her rubber gloves. He unpeeled a plastic garbage bag from the roll and returned to the piano for Aubie.

After depositing the cat's body in the garbage can beside the garage, Hardy went back inside the house. There, he threw open some more windows and got a big fan down out of the top of the closet.

He went back to Millie in the car, where he found her pale and shaky, clutching a shredded tissue to her mouth and nose.

"Honey, it's Aubie. He's gone."

"Oh, no. Poor fella. How did he die? Where?"

"I guess old age. You know he'd been slowing down lately, getting too fat. I found him on the floor in front of the windows where he used to chatter at the birds on the feeder outside. I don't think he suffered."

"What did you do with him?"

"I just wrapped him up temporarily, but I'll find a nice spot in the garden for a grave. But, honey, I don't think you need to stay in the house tonight until it's completely aired out. I'm going to run you over to Jabo's. The beds are still made up. Just order in some food if you feel like eating. I'm going to come back here and clean up some more and bury Aubie."

"But Hardy…"

"Just do as I say Millie, okay? Everything will be alright."

*   *   *   *

Once back from settling Millie at Jabo's, Hardy fished his .44 Magnum out from under the front seat of the car and cautiously re-entered the reeking house. He never would have been able to explain the yanked out kitchen cabinet drawers, the dumped contents of the desk or the ransacked dresser drawers to Millie without alarming her. In her weakened condition she must never know the danger he had brought down on them. It was too late to hope the nightmare was ending.

CHAPTER 27

▼

After Millie heard the garage door open and Hardy drive off, she got out of bed and showered. Hardy didn't think she was well enough to drive. Christmas was almost here, and she was going shopping.

She slipped into blue Auburn warm-ups and jogging shoes. In front of the bathroom mirror she sighed as she twisted the short fuzzy wisps of what was once her luxurious mane and finally gave up on trying to style it. She scrounged through the top of Hardy's closet until she came up with one of his old ball caps and jammed it snuggly down on top of her ears.

The extra key to the Jeep was in Hardy's dresser drawer.

A slow, cold drizzle leaked from the dark clouds. She turned on her low beams and wipers and played with the radio dial, locking in Elvis's *Blue Christmas.* The traffic was heavy with last-minute shoppers. If Hardy found out she had driven to Huntsville by herself, he'd freak. And if she put a scratch on his precious Wagoneer, well, he'd freak some more.

The speedometer registered 55 when a Nativity scene in a churchyard on her left caught her attention. Just as she turned to look, her peripheral vision saw an object moving up beside her. A blue Chevy veered dangerously close to the driver's side. Millie scowled at the driver, motioning for him to get back into his own lane. The elderly driver in turn motioned for her to pull over.

"God, what does this old creep want?," she cried out loud. There was no way she was going to pull over on this lonely stretch of road without another car in sight. Just then the blue car pulled slightly ahead and swerved into her left front fender, trying to cut her off.

She slammed the brakes and jerked the steering wheel hard right in an effort to miss it and the Jeep spun sideways, sliding out of control toward a concrete culvert.

"Oh my God!" She felt a hard bump as the vehicle rolled over something, then heard a loud thud beneath the undercarriage. Suddenly she was airborne. Her flight lasted an eternity. She thought about Clint and Hardy and how they would have Christmas. She landed with a jolting crash that sent a shock wave up her spine and it felt like her lower teeth bit into her eye sockets. She felt instant pain. Light faded and she smelled cabbage cooking in her grandmother's kitchen and the sweet aroma of her grandfather's pipe tobacco. She felt the warmth of her mother's breast, the firmness of her father's hand as he held her in his lap and tied her shoes, the first time she and Hardy made love in the back seat of his '57 Chevy, giving birth.

But her last thought was how pissed Hardy would be when he learned she had wrecked his Wagoneer.

✶   ✶   ✶   ✶

Hardy barged through the automatic door into the ER and rushed to the cubicle where Millie lay on a bloody sheet. An IV extended from her arm. A nurse was threading a tube down her throat. A young doctor in green scrubs was yelling orders.

"Sir, you can't come in here!" a nurse said.

But Hardy wasn't listening. He grabbed Millie's free hand, squeezing it and leaning over her.

"Millie, sweetheart! I'm here."

"Sir, please!" said a nurse.

"Oh God, Millie, talk to me. Say something! Please say something!"

But all he heard was gurgling. He moved toward her head and saw the doctor nod to the nurses and they made no move to stop him. Hardy stroked the short, blonde stubble covering her scalp. He whispered in her ear as he stroked her head, "I love you darling. Squeeze back." No response. "Millie, please don't leave me," he sobbed. "Oh God. Millie. I love you."

* * * *

From his motel room, Klaus called Herman Blucker in Interlaken, Switzerland. "Herr Blucker, I have located the person who listed the reichsmarks for sale."

"Are you sure?"

"*Ja.*"

"If he has the reichsmarks, the Fuhrer document must be nearby," Blucker said.

"*Ja.*"

"You know what to do. And do it quickly."

Chapter 28

Ben Wasserman looked at the calendar on his desk a second time and counted off the days to April 20th. There were only 90 remaining. He gathered documents and stuffed them into his brown leather briefcase and flicked off the desk lamp. It was only 3 p.m., but he wasn't feeling well. Since noon he had been hacking and running a low-grade fever. Now, he ached. Probably the flu.

He didn't have time to be sick. The AG, he surmised, would work out an immunity deal with Sunny Webber and her attorney, but it could take days, even weeks.

What if the information Sunny promised to give didn't finger Raven? Then what? The thought made his stomach move up in his throat.

He wound his woolen scarf around his neck, slipped into his topcoat and headed for the door. The phone rang.

"Damn." For a second, he decided to keep walking. But discipline and habit prevailed. He answered. It was Fletcher Preston in Huntsville.

"I was curious about the status of Sunny Webber's immunity request," Preston said.

"It's in the mill." Ben coughed and slumped down at his desk. "It's being reviewed at the highest levels."

"Tell me something," Preston said. "Why is Justice willing to consider immunity for a drug trafficker just because she happens to know someone who was a baby Nazi?"

"I can't tell you any more than what you heard Sunny Webber say at the jail."

"You sound awful."

"I'm coming down with the flu."

"I've got some information you can chew on while you recuperate."

"What's that?"

"I've checked with the postal employees in Huntsville and it appears that Joe Smith is an alias. They say the mail was picked up by an old drunk named Doolittle who lived across the street in a fleabag motel."

"Did you talk to him?"

"I attempted to." Preston paused. "But dead men can't talk."

The words came like a shot of adrenaline. "Tell me!"

"I don't know a whole lot at this time, other than Doolittle was found dead in his room. The HPD thinks someone roughed him up before he died. They're keeping the case under wraps, hoping the killer will attempt to pick up the mail."

"Do they have any leads?" Ben asked.

"Maybe. The place had been wiped clean, but they did find a print on the wall."

"Any matches?"

"Not yet," Preston said. "I understand that it's been sent to the National Crime Lab in D.C."

"Keep me posted." Ben said, "And thanks."

"You bet. And Ben?"

"Yes?"

"Drink about four fingers of Jack Black and go to bed. If it doesn't cure the flu, at least you won't give a damn."

"Thanks. Call me if you get any matches on the print."

"Count on it."

Chapter 29

▼

Sylvia Birch knew who was calling.

"Hi, this is Sylvia. Sorry I can't come to the phone. Please leave a message at the tone."

"Sylvia, if you're there, pick up. It's important that I speak with you. Please don't cut me off."

Rudy's voice sounded urgent. But his call was too late. Her mind was made up.

"I confess I haven't been very attentive…and I have been gone a lot. I accept all of the blame. It's all my fault. And yes, I did have an affair. So there you are. But it was just sex. I don't love her. I love you. I am very, very sorry for the pain I've caused you." His voice trailed off. "If you are there, please pick up. I don't see why we have to communicate through attorneys. This is our problem, not theirs."

Sylvia sat up in bed and looked at the phone. What did he take her for? If he admitted to having the French exchange student once, he probably had her a dozen times. And what about other women? "Screw you," she muttered.

"I know what you're thinking," he said. "I promise you, it was a one-time thing and I realize what a big mistake I made."

She jerked up the phone and shouted into the receiver. "Liar! And don't call again!" She slammed down the phone and sat back against the headboard, shaking.

The phone rang again and the answering machine clicked on. "Darling, I don't blame you for being angry. You have every right to be. No matter what you may think, I am telling the truth. Please pick up. What harm is there in talking to me?"

Sylvia thought for a moment. She wanted to give him a piece of her mind. She was tempted to answer. He sounded sincere. She was paralyzed with indecision.

"Darling, I'm really hurting. I can't go on like this. Please pick up."

She reached for the receiver.

"What do you want?" Her voice quavered.

"Thank God. I just wanted to hear your voice. Are you okay?"

"Yes. Now you listen to me. You have hurt me deeply. I believed in you, Rudy, and you have betrayed me."

"You are absolutely right. And I am ashamed."

"I don't know that I can ever get over what you've done."

"You have every right to be angry at me." he said. "What I have done to you is unforgivable, but I beg you to forgive me. Darling, I don't want a divorce. I want you."

She felt her resolve ebbing.

"I'm confused," she said. "I don't want to make any decisions about anything at the moment."

"And you don't have to," Rudy said. "All I'm asking for is a chance to show you that I have changed. This has been a wake-up call for me. I'll go to counseling, I'll do whatever I have to do to keep our relationship intact. I want to grow old with you. Just give me a chance. That's all that I ask."

"I don't know that I could ever trust you again."

"Staying together and resolving our problems is a start. The trust will come when you know I mean it."

"You make it sound so simple."

"It is, darling—if we work together."

"I just don't know."

"Will you at least give me a chance? If it doesn't work out, then we'll get a divorce. Okay?"

"I don't know."

"Darling, you don't know how happy you have made me."

"There is one question I have to ask," she said.

"Certainly."

"How many times did you have sex with the other woman?"

"Only once. I promise."

"But why? I thought it was good between us, especially the sex."

"It was. You're the best," said Rudy, his voice dropping to a soft, liquid caress. "I've never felt anything with anyone else like I've felt with you. She didn't mean anything to me. She wasn't' even very imaginative, not like you."

"Rudy, I don't need to hear this...I've got to work through this, and it may take time."

"I understand," Rudy said. "But I do hope I can see you."

After hanging up, she resumed reading her novel, but couldn't concentrate and finally put it down. She never wanted a divorce. Rudy was an exciting lover and what had hurt so deeply was catching him with another woman, and in their own river cabin. The thought of it still made her ill. Yet, Rudy had admitted his infidelity. Most men would have lied. If he said it was a one-time thing, she didn't know that it wasn't.

She swung out of bed and went to the vanity and sat in front of the mirror and brushed her blonde hair. Tomorrow, she would invest in a new hairstyle and have her nails done.

* * * *

The back road between Huntsville and Nashville wound through rolling hill country and past neat farms where cattle and horses grazed behind white plank fences. For late January, the weather was warm, the sky a hazy blue. Rudy slid back the sunroof of the BMW and inserted a disc in the CD player, Mozart's *Don Giovanni*.

Sylvia winced. She hadn't heard the piece since that night she stood outside the river cabin.

"Can we listen to something else?"

"I thought you loved this." He pushed his sunglasses against the bridge of his nose.

"Please, just don't play it."

Rudy pressed the eject button.

After a moment she turned to Rudy and said, "May I ask you a question?"

"Anything."

"Do you promise that you really love me?"

Rudy smiled. "With all my heart."

Sylvia reached over and removed his sunglasses.

"Now say it again." She looked deep into his brown eyes.

"With all my heart."

She sighed and relaxed her head against the headrest. "What a gorgeous day."

"Yes, and what a gorgeous woman you are," Rudy said. He reached over and took her hand in his and squeezed it gently. "Why are you smiling?"

"This reminds me of when we first became lovers."

"We had some really great times, didn't we?"

"Yes."

"There's no reason it can't be that way again." Rudy pulled her gently toward him and placed a hand on her thigh, stroking and gradually moving up.

Sylvia stiffened.

"What's wrong?" Rudy asked.

"I'm not ready for that."

"I understand," Rudy said.

"I just mean, let's not rush things," she added. "Do you understand?"

"Certainly, darling."

Rudy was especially handsome today, she thought. The brown slacks and matching sweater were her favorites.

"Where are we going?" she asked.

"Nashville."

"Overnight?" she said, surprised.

"Maybe."

"Why didn't you tell me? I didn't bring a thing, not even a toothbrush."

"That would have destroyed the spontaneity," Rudy said. "Isn't it more fun to be surprised? Anyway, if you need something, I'll buy it."

She smiled again.

"Now what?" Rudy asked.

"Remember the time you called and told me to meet you at the airport in one hour?"

"And the next thing you know, we were on a plane to..."

"Paris. It was my favorite trip. God, we had fun."

"It was the best."

"I do love you." Rudy suddenly swerved up the exit ramp. He pulled in at a liquor store and left the engine running.

"I'll be right back," he said and disappeared inside the store.

Sylvia rested her head on the back of the seat and closed her eyes. *How can life be so shitty one moment and so great the next?*

Rudy returned with a bottle of champagne in a Styrofoam bucket of ice. He placed it on the leather seat between them and produced two long-stemmed plastic flutes.

"What are you doing?"

"The occasion calls for champagne." Rudy opened the bottle and poured her glass full, then filled his.

"You're crazy," Sylvia said. "If we're stopped, you'll be arrested."

"My, you are getting cautious, aren't you? Sometimes we have to live on the edge, like the old days," he said. "Now for a toast: To our future. May it be filled with love and good times."

"Yes," Sylvia said, lifting her glass and touching his.

Rudy pulled onto the road and headed toward Nashville.

After her first glass of champagne she was more relaxed and less guarded. She had to admit she was enjoying herself.

"I must be honest with you," she said, looking at Rudy. "When you called me to ask me out, I had reservations."

"I understand."

"I'm having a good time. Thank you." She leaned across the seat and kissed him on the cheek.

"I'm glad I called," he said.

"Can we ever go back and recapture the old days?"

"No, but we can make the new days better."

After checking in at the Hyatt in Nashville, they stepped into a glass elevator off the cavernous lobby. Rudy punched the tenth floor button and the glass bubble shot upward.

Sylvia clutched Rudy's arm with both hands and squeezed her eyes shut.

"I hate these things," she said. "You know how afraid of heights I am."

Rudy wrapped his arm around her shoulder and pulled her against him. "It's okay," he said.

* * * *

The room was large and done up in blossom pink with a king-size bed. In a sitting area were a couch, two overstuffed chairs and coffee table. Rudy pulled back the drapes, revealing the silver skyline of Nashville, the Cumberland River below and rolling hills undulating to the northwest.

"Would you look at that view!" he said.

Later, they went to dinner at a revolving restaurant on the top floor of the hotel. Sylvia refused to sit near the glass wall that offered a panoramic view of city lights. They ended up in the coffee shop off the lobby eating turkey sandwiches.

"When you fly you aren't afraid," Rudy said.

"It's different." Sylvia sipped her white wine. "Sorry I spoiled our dinner plans."

"It's no loss. The important thing is that I'm with you."

Sylvia looked into her wine and turned the goblet by the stem.

"What are you thinking?" Rudy asked.

Sylvia looked at him, studying his eyes. "You really want to know?"

"Yes."

"Maybe I shouldn't say it," she said.

"Why not?"

"I was thinking, is this for real, or is Rudy treating me like this for a reason?"

Rudy reached across the table and placed his hand on hers. "Both," he said. "It is real. And the reason is because I love you."

* * * *

Inside the room, Rudy pointed the remote at the TV and channel-surfed while Sylvia disappeared into the bathroom. Several minutes later, she emerged.

"Turn around," she said.

Rudy turned around. She was standing in the doorway in a sheer pale blue wrapper, open down the front.

Chapter 30

The Attorney General appeared older than when Ben Wasserman had last seen her. She looked tired. But her handshake was firm. Behind the thick lenses, her dark eyes looked as large as bottle caps.

"Ben, it's nice to see you. I apologize for asking you to come at a late hour, but after receiving your memo, I wanted to meet with you as quickly as possible."

The AG gestured toward a sitting area in one corner of the spacious room where a blue couch faced two matching easy chairs. She took a seat in one of the chairs and Ben sat on the couch. She reached for a file on a nearby table.

"I have read with great interest your report on Magdalene Webber. The woman obviously possesses information that is critical to our investigation," she said. "Whether it is enough to lead us to Raven, I don't know. The woman is very shrewd. She gave us just enough information to whet our appetites."

Ben nodded.

"As you already know, I can't—I won't just grant immunity from prosecution in the trafficking cases. The request must originate with the U.S. Attorney's office in Northern Alabama and move up the proper channels." She coughed into her fist and continued. "I can cut through bureaucratic red tape if I choose and expedite the request for immunity, but I don't want to be left hanging out to dry if this story turns out to be bogus."

"I understand, General."

"If the woman is credible, I don't mind sticking my neck out. I wasn't there to observe her. Is she a crackpot or not?"

"General, the woman looked me squarely in the eyes and I believed her. Special FBI Agent Fletcher Preston was also present. He believes her."

"When one is facing life in prison, I suppose one can become very convincing," she said.

"True."

"What would prevent her from concocting the entire story? Or, for that matter repeating something she had heard?"

"Only someone present at the time would know these details."

"Yes, I suppose you're right," she said. "I'm so desperate to locate Raven, I'm afraid I will believe any cock 'n bull story. We must be careful, Ben. A lot is riding on us bringing this matter to a quick and successful resolution. There isn't a week that passes that the director of National Security doesn't call me. The President's chief of staff called yesterday. You have no idea how much pressure I'm under. Don't let me down on this."

Ben twisted on the couch. His bum leg ached. "General, it would be helpful if I knew the reason I am searching for Raven."

"Yes, I think it's time you know why you have been given this mission." The AG leaned forward in the chair and crossed her feet. Her tired eyes narrowed. "What I'm about to tell you is so sensitive that you can't even dream about it. Understand?"

"Yes."

"Adolf Hitler and Eva Braun were lovers for many years. She spent much of her time at the Berghof, Hitler's mountain retreat overlooking Berchtesgaden. What was not known, until after the Berlin wall fell and East German Secret Police records were available, was that Hitler and Eva Braun had a child."

Ben felt his muscle involuntarily quiver at the corner of his mouth.

"I see that you're just as surprised as I was when I first heard about it," the AG said.

"Yes, but it's logical."

"Even though Hitler inflicted unspeakable evil upon the world, he didn't want the German people to know he was living in sin with a woman. He certainly didn't want the German people to know he had fathered a child out of wedlock."

"I suppose it might have tarnished his sterling image."

"I'm puzzled why our government is concerned that this child gained illegal entry into the country," Ben said. "People come here illegally every day. It would be good politics, I suppose, if we locate Hitler's child and deport him."

"I wish it were that simple. But it's far more complex and dangerous. They will kill anyone who stands in their way."

"They?"

"The Raven Group." The AG's lowered her voice. "Let me start at the beginning. According to the SSD records, the child's nanny, Ava Mueller, was captured by the Russians at the end of the war. During her interrogation, it was learned that she'd been part of Hitler's inner circle at the Berghof. She spilled everything to the Russian interrogators.

"The Russians set out to find the boy, and concluded that he had been spirited out of the country. Now, we know that he was sneaked into this country posing as a child of parents who were members of the German rocket team. He's been here for years growing, gathering strength, just waiting for the day."

"But why?"

"Neo-Nazism, as you well know, is on the rise in Germany. The Raven Group, unlike Odessa, which is primarily dedicated to protecting former SS members, is a shadowy band of hard core SS members believed to have at their disposal large sums of money on deposit in Swiss bank accounts. Their aim is to regain power in Germany."

She leaned closer. "The CIA has learned that Raven—the code name for Hitler's heir, Wolfgang—is planning to return to Germany and make his debut on April 20th, Hitler's birthday. This is before the general elections. Can you imagine the electrifying effect this could have on old Nazis and the current crop of skinheads, malcontents and just plain fringe nutcases? Such an event could skewer the election results—not enough, of course, to win but enough to get a toehold. Germany is in an economic downturn. When the Wall came down and the country was reunified, the cost was massive. They raised taxes—already high—to cover the cost. Production is down, unemployment is double digit and the country is in the throes of a recession. Crime is up, as well as emigration. People are dissatisfied. The country is ripe for change."

"Not back to Nazism."

"Don't forget Ben, that when Hitler rose to power in the '30s, Germany was a leader in music and science; the country of Martin Luther, Kant, Goethe, Bach, Beethoven and Brahms. It was a great cultural center of the world. No one thought Nazism could happen then. But it did."

The new knowledge weighed heavily on his shoulders.

"And if I do find him?"

"That problem will be resolved by means which I'm not at liberty to discuss."

"If I can't?"

"Our government will not sit idly by and permit the Nazis to regain power in Germany."

* * * *

Ben ate the last slice of pizza, then dumped the empty box in the trash can. Lately, eating dinner at the office had become the norm. He poured a stale cup of coffee and returned to his cluttered desk and looked at the calendar. Only seventeen days. Sunny Webber had clammed up and refused to talk until the terms of her immunity had been signed and sealed. Her lawyer haggled over the details.

The phone on his desk rang. He picked up. "Wasserman."

"Don't you ever take a break?" It was Preston.

"Not anymore."

"I have some info. I don't know if it will be any help, but you did ask me to stay in touch."

"What have you got?"

"A match on that print."

Ben's brain didn't compute. "Jog my memory."

"The one lifted in that fleabag motel where the old drunk was found dead."

"Oh, yeah." Ben grabbed a legal pad and clicked his ballpoint.

"It belongs to a lawyer in French Springs, a small town west of Huntsville."

"Got a name?"

"Yeah. James Hardy Jackson. Small town lawyer, age 43, recently widowed, played football at Auburn, well-liked around town. Good citizen type."

"Has Huntsville PD questioned him?" Ben asked.

"Not yet. They're keeping him under surveillance for the time being."

"Keep me posted, will you?"

"Sure."

"Thanks for the tip."

Ben rose from behind his desk and walked to the window, hands clasped behind his back, and stared into the night, mulling over the latest bit of information. He recounted in his mind what he knew. Someone using a Huntsville post office box and calling himself "Joe Smith" had listed the reichsmarks for sale with Sterling Auction. Yet, it was an old man named Doolittle that had accessed the box. Why the subterfuge? Doolittle had turned up dead. Now this lawyer's fingerprints were found in the dead man's room.

He returned to his desk and buzzed the unit secretary. "Roberta, get a rundown on James Hardy Jackson. White male, age 43, from French Springs, Alabama. I want to know everything about him: who his parents are, down to what he eats for breakfast. And don't waste any time."

Chapter 31

▼

A cold drizzle was falling when Hardy emerged from his law office around 9:30 p.m., and locked the front door. He hefted the .44 magnum deeper in his pocket. He rattled the latch twice, making sure it was locked, looked quickly up and down Joe Wheeler Street, and dashed to the Thunderbird parked in the handicapped space. Downtown French Springs was deserted. The empty asphalt glistened like yellow satin ribbons under the streetlights. He clicked his keyless entry, glanced in the backseat, then slid into the car and punched the door lock. He turned the ignition and scanned the radio dial until a country music station came up. He suddenly remembered he hadn't eaten since lunch. He wasn't hungry, but the thought of going home to an empty house was unthinkable. Since Millie's death he had been working longer hours, doing anything to fill the day. He backed out and headed for Waffle House near the interstate.

* * * *

Klaus Kluge cruised Beauregard Street checking out the neighborhood, circled the block once, returned and parked the blue Chevy beneath a huge oak tree, well away from the nearest street light. He killed the engine and headlights and sat for a full minute. He slid out of the car, closed the door softly, and hurried along the sidewalk toward a two-story white clapboard with a garage on the side. It was the old section of town. Metal historic markers proclaiming construction date and past and current owners dotted well-manicured lawns. When he reached a marker that read "1905 Wilson-Jackson House," he turned in and walked along the edge of tall shrubs and around to the garage where the door was up. No lights on. He swept a hand back over his face and head to wipe the rain away, removed a flashlight from his coat pocket and stabbed the beam around the garage. Lawnmower, ladder and sacks of pine bark in the corner. Tools on one wall. He went to the door that led inside the house and twisted the knob. Locked. From the tool board, he took a flathead screwdriver and wedged it between the door and jam and jimmied back the plunger until the door popped open.

Inside, he crept through the dark. Next, he made his way through the other rooms on the ground floor—dining room, living room and den. A carpeted staircase lead to the second floor. He shined the light to the top of the stairs, then climbed. Boards creaked under his weight. He cursed under his breath.

A clock chimed 10 somewhere near the front door.

* * * *

Hardy drove into the darkened garage and sat in the car for several seconds looking around before pressing the electronic door device clipped to his visor. The door groaned and rattled downward. He killed the headlights and engine and slid from the car and walked in the dark a few feet to the door, which he found unlocked. God, how could he have forgotten to close the garage door this morning *and* leave the door unlocked? He had been so fried lately. He pushed open the door and turned on the inside light as he stepped into the kitchen. The place was a mess. Dirty dishes were stacked high in the sink and the butter he had forgotten to put up had melted and oozed onto the counter. He'd clean it up tomorrow. He was too tired tonight.

Hardy trudged up the stairs and down the long hallway to the master bedroom.

He flicked on the overhead light, removed the revolver from his pocket and placed it under a pillow on the bed. Peeling off his wet trench coat, he draped it across the back of a chair. After stripping down to his boxer shorts, he padded down the hallway to the guest bathroom—he still hadn't gotten around to fixing the commode in the master bath. He brushed, flossed and peed before returning to the bedroom. After clicking on the TV, he straightened the bedcovers and crawled between the sheets. He reached over and took the framed picture of Millie from the bedside table and traced the outline of her face with his fingertip.

* * * *

Hardy awoke with a start. An old black and white movie was playing on TV. Millie's photo lay face down on his chest. He clicked off the TV, replaced the picture on the nightstand and lay still for a long time. He was certain he had heard a noise coming from the hallway.

He slowly turned from his back, onto his left side, facing the open bedroom door. The house was quiet. Only the soft humming of the heat pump could be heard over the thumping of his heart. He mentally reviewed every door and window in the house. Were they locked? Yes, he had checked them. Had he lowered the garage door and locked the kitchen door? Yeah. Tomorrow, he would have dead-bolt locks installed on every door in the house.

The revolver just under the pillow provided a measure of security.

Then a blinding light struck him in the face.

Hardy's hand shot to his face to shield from the glare. "Who—who are you? What do you want?" But he knew this was no crackhead after money.

"Ver is the document?"

"I don't know what you're talking about."

"I know you have the reichsmarks. The document is nearby."

"At the office...in—in the safe."

"Ve vill go get it."

"I need to dress, put on my shoes..."

"I haff you now, Mr. Jackson. You've been a hard case, I must say. First, you give me the slip at the railway and then when I think I haff you again, it turns out to be your wife. Tch, tch, typical woman driver. But it is too bad she wound up dead. Our business wasn't with her."

His words were a hot, searing iron plunged deep into Hardy's brain. Millie had not died in a freak accident on a slippery highway. They were after him. The rotten son of a bitch had killed Millie. Rage boiled up as sour bile in his throat. Blind hatred replaced all logic. He would kill the Nazi bastard if he died trying.

Hardy's hand shot under the pillow and closed over cold steel and he whirled toward the door. The flashlight beam stabbed him in the face! He aimed just above the light. The big revolver barked, almost jumping from his hand as a blaze of fire spewed from the muzzle. He dropped to the floor, heard gunfire and felt the wake of a bullet whiz past his ear and heard glass shattering. He gripped the pistol with both hands to steady his aim, fired again, and again. The room was thick with the acrid smell of gunpowder. He heard a groan and the flashlight banged to the floor and went dark. Footsteps pounded down the hallway, then creaking stair boards. Hardy jumped to his feet and ran out into the darkened hallway and fired another round in the direction of the fleeing footsteps.

"You son of a bitch!" He was wild with hatred. The kitchen door to the garage slammed and he heard the garage door rumble open. Hardy ran toward the sound. He jerked open the door and peered out into the darkened garage. The man was running down the driveway toward the street. Hardy darted out of the house to see the man silhouetted in the glow of streetlights. Stepping onto the sidewalk, he aimed his gun at the fleeing figure and fired. The big revolver bucked. Missed. He fired again. The man jumped into a car. Hardy kept pulling the trigger, but there were only clicks.

Lights flicked on up and down the street. Hardy stood trembling on the sidewalk, the revolver hanging at his side. A wave of nausea swept through him and he felt weak. He gagged and ran toward the house. He made it as far as the garage before he doubled over.

* * * *

The rain had stopped and the moon was peeking through the clouds when Hardy reached the turn-off at Taylor's cotton gin in the north part of the county. He killed the headlights and pulled behind the two-story tin building. He parked out of sight, between two metal cotton wagons and left the motor idling while he looked around. The reloaded Smith and Wesson, lay on the seat beside him. Satisfied that he hadn't been followed, he called Sarah. It was 2 a.m. She answered after the fifth ring.

"Hell-o." Her voice was heavy with sleep.

"Sarah?"

"Who is this? Hardy!"

"Someone—a man with a German accent—broke into my house tonight."

"Oh my God!" She came fully awake. "What did he want?"

"The document."

"My God!"

"Get a grip and listen."

"If he knows where you live, he knows where I live."

"I know that. Wake Jasmine and go directly to the county jail. You'll be safe there. Don't tell Sheriff Horsely about the document."

"What'll I say?"

"He already knows that something went down at my house—the shooting and all. Someone called the cops. I heard sirens when I was driving away. Tell him a burglar broke into my house, that I chased him and I'm out looking for him. He may be wounded and he's probably driving a blue Chevy."

"Where are you?" Sarah asked.

"Taylor's gin. It's near the old Tuten plantation."

"I know the place."

"I'll be safe here until I can figure out what to do," he said.

* * * *

Klaus Kluge bent over the lavatory in his grimy motel room and ran cold water over the wound on his left forearm. The bullet had sliced open the flesh, leaving a nasty gash, but didn't appear to have damaged any major vessels. He cleaned the wound thoroughly and wrapped it with a towel. Later, he would buy an antiseptic ointment and dressing, but first he must make a phone call. He sat on the edge of the bed, fired a cigarette, then called Hermann Blucker in Interlaken.

"Herr Blucker, I have finally located the document you have been searching for."

"That is good news."

"However, the owner is reluctant to part with it."

"I follow what you're saying. Tell me what to do."

"Perhaps, someone more persuasive would be useful."

"What about Heinz? And then there is our young American friend we can call on."

"Excellent."

"I'll make sure he comes on the very next flight."

* * * *

The roar of car tires slinging gravel woke Hardy. He sat inside the gin where morning sunlight poured through a window, his back against a pile of unginned cotton. He jumped to his feet and ran to the window and peeked out. It was Sarah's gray Volvo. "Shit! What's she doing here?"

She drove around to the back of the gin and skidded to a stop. He watched as she hurried toward the door, carrying a small paper sack. He wedged the pistol behind his belt and held open the door for her.

"You shouldn't be here," he growled. "It's too dangerous."

"I brought you something to eat." She withdrew a sausage and biscuit and handed it to him.

"Thanks, but I'm not hungry."

"When trouble comes in it's deuces," she said.

"What are you talking about?"

"Two cops were waiting at the office when I arrived this morning."

"About what happened at the house?"

"No, they were from Huntsville P.D., looking for you."

"Damn!" His stomach churned. "What did they want?"

"Didn't say. They wanted to know where they could find you."

"Are you sure they were cops?"

"Yeah."

"What did you tell them?"

"That you had taken a few days off work and had gone out of town."

"Good." He walked off a few paces. "I don't know what to do. Cops are coming from one direction, Nazi's from the other."

"And both will be back."

"I know. I'm not afraid of the cops. All they'll do is arrest me."

"Please get rid of that document."

Hardy pulled Sarah to his chest, feeling her body tremble. "I've already thought of that."

"Then give them what they want."

"I can't."

"Why?"

"The document will keep us alive. If I give it to them, they'll kill us for sure. As long as we have what they want, they won't harm us."

Sarah looked up at Hardy, her eyes filled with fear. "What are we going to do in the meantime? You can't hide here forever. And Jasmine…" She began to sob.

"Is there some place that you can take her until this blows over?"

Sarah wiped her eyes. "I'll think of something. What about you?"

"I can stay at Pop's house until I think of some place better."

"Please be careful, Hardy."

"I will. And you be careful, too. We'll get through this."

Chapter 32

The telephone buzzed. Wasserman picked it up. It was the AG.

"An immunity agreement and witness protection plan has been finalized between Sunny Webber and the government," she said without preliminary.

"Did she give us the name?"

"She will as soon as you get down to Huntsville."

"I'll catch the next flight out."

"After this Webber woman gives you the name, I want you to corroborate her story. I don't intend to be made a fool. If her story checks out, we go ahead. If not, there is no deal. You have at your disposal the FBI office in Huntsville. They are expecting you."

"I understand," said Ben.

"Notify me immediately where Wolfgang Hitler can be located. I will take over from that point. Divulge your mission to no one. Understand?"

"Yes, General."

"I'll be waiting on your call."

*   *   *   *

Preston was waiting for Ben at Huntsville International. Soon, they were driving toward town.

"The word is that the U.S. Attorney has cut a deal with Sunny Webber," said Preston.

"That's correct."

"And protection."

"Right again." Ben said.

She must know a helluva lot about someone."

Yup," said Ben.

Yeah, I received direct orders from Washington this morning, practically turning my whole damn office over to you. So tell me where may I drive you, your Lordship?"

The county jail."

* * * *

Billy Joe Carlton, briefcase in hand, was waiting at the jailer station when Ben and Preston stepped off the elevator.

The same corpulent jailer was on duty. He had the complexion of a slab of pork. "Ya'll hafta sign in," he said.

The men dutifully signed the register.

The jailer picked up a large key ring and wobbled off. "Ya'll follow me."

In the same small room as before, the men scraped back chairs and seated themselves. Ben rested one arm on the tabletop and nervously drummed. Down the corridor, he heard footsteps squeaking on polished concrete. They grew louder. He sat up and turned to face the entrance. The door creaked open and a small woman with cropped brown hair and a sunken face, wearing orange coveralls, stepped inside. Except for the dark circles under her eyes, she looked like an exhumed corpse. Ben hardly recognized her.

Carlton stood up and pulled out a chair for her. "Are they treating you okay?" he asked.

"Oh, it's been a nonstop party."

"Of course, you know Mr. Wasserman and Mr. Preston," the lawyer said.

Sunny nodded.

"I understand you have a name for me," Ben said.

"I've been thinking about something, Mr. Wasserman."

"What's that?"

"Our agreement states that the government will furnish me with a new identity, a new Social Security card, driver license, credit card and relocate me and help me find a job."

"That's right."

"But who will protect me from the government?"

"As long as you cooperate and give testimony in the trafficking cases, you have nothing to fear."

"I'm not referring to that. I'm talking about the name. The way I figure it, once the government gets the name, they won't want me around."

"Your fear is wholly unfounded. As long as you cooperate and remain in the program you'll be safe."

She looked Ben straight in the eye. "You appear to be a nice man, Mr. Wasserman, but perhaps a bit naive."

Ben ignored her comment and opened his briefcase and removed a legal pad and pen. He tore off a piece of paper and slid it and the pen across the table to Sunny Webber. "The name, please."

She picked up the ballpoint and clicked it and scribbled something on the paper, and slid it back across the table to him, face down.

"You've got what you wanted. Now get me out of here."

He picked up the paper, and looked at the name. It meant nothing to him.

"Do you know where this individual lives?" he asked.

"In the area."

Ben placed the paper in the briefcase and snapped it shut. "My instructions are to corroborate your story. When I'm satisfied that you're telling the truth, you'll be transferred."

On the way down in the elevator to the sally port, Ben took out a card and wrote a name on the back and gave it to Preston. "Locate this individual and check his background."

"When do you need it?"

"Last week."

* * * *

Klaus Kluge stood near the large glass windows at Huntsville International, squinting into the morning sun, watching as the Delta 727 rolled to a stop. Shortly, sleepy-eyed passengers poured into the terminal. Klaus scanned the approaching faces. Towering above everyone else was a large, bald man wearing a black turtleneck sweater and black leather coat. Heinz Quackernach was a bull of a man. Even at age 73.

Klaus stepped forward and extended his hand at the same time a tough looking punk arose from a chair across the concourse and also made his way toward Heinz.

"How vas your flight?"

"Very tiring," Heinz said enveloping Klaus' hand. And then turning toward the leather-jacketed, heavy-set man who hovered nearby, "Frederick, I presume? I recognized you from your photo."

At a quizzical look from Kluge, Quackernach introduced the thirtyish man with shaved head as "our American friend."

After retrieving his baggage, Heinz squeezed into the front seat of the rental car and Klaus drove west across the flat farmland.

"Tell me about our other American friend," Heinz said.

"Jackson's his name—a lawyer."

Heinz shifted his bulk in the seat. "That vill make it more pleasurable."

"Don't underestimate him. He's armed and full of fight. I am fortunate that I escaped with only a flesh wound."

"Ver is he?"

"Hiding out. He hasn't been in his office or home since our unfortunate meeting."

"Vat is your pleasure, kamerad?"

"First, ve find him," Klaus said. "Then ve begin breaking his bones one at a time until he tells us ver the Fuhrer document is located."

"Yes. A good plan."

Chapter 33

"What did you say?" Hardy pressed the phone to his ear.

"The Department of Justice, Office of Special Investigation," Sarah whispered.

"Where?"

"Here, at the office. Just outside my door."

"What does he want?"

"To speak with you."

"About what?"

"He didn't say, only that it's a matter of great urgency. Those were his words."

"You didn't tell him where?"

"Of course not."

"How do you know he's legit?"

"He showed me his credentials. He has Fed stamped all over him. Close-clipped gray hair, gray suit, gray everything."

"What do you think?"

"It won't hurt to talk."

"What's his name?"

"Wasserman."

"Put him on."

Hardy waited for what seemed an eternity. He'd bet his life it was about the reichsmarks.

"Good afternoon, Mr. Jackson. How are you?" The voice sounded friendly.

"What do you want?"

"I like your directness, Mr. Jackson. It's imperative that I meet with you immediately."

"What about?"

"Nine million reichsmarks. You are the one who listed them with Sterling Auctions?"

"Maybe. I was representing a client. And that's privileged information. I think I've said too much already."

"The government has no interest in prosecuting you, Mr. Jackson. I assure you."

"What's the point?"

"To meet with you immediately."

"I'll give it some thought."

"There is no time for dilly-dallying, Mr. Jackson. Many lives may hang in the balance."

Hardy swallowed hard. I know a place," he said. "What kind of car are you driving?"

"A green Ford, a rental."

"Take 157 east for about four miles; turn north on blacktop, go two miles and turn right onto a gravel road that leads to a cemetery. I'll meet you there in one hour. Come alone."

* * * *

Jackson Cemetery was located off the main road on a swell of land that offered an unobstructed view in all directions. A narrow gravel road was the only access. Hardy drove past the entrance and continued north several hundred yards to where an abandoned farmhouse sat on a high knoll. It had once been his grandfather's home. He pulled around to the back and parked beneath a copse of cedars where he had a clear view of the cemetery and the surrounding area. He picked up binoculars that had belonged to his father and swept the landscape from right to left until he was satisfied that no one else was around. He removed the .44 from the glove compartment and placed it on the seat beside him. Outside, it was cold and the iron gray clouds promised rain. He turned up the heater, waited and worried. Precisely at 3:30 p.m. a car turned off the asphalt and moved slowly up the gravel road toward the cemetery. Hardy grabbed the binoculars. It was a green Ford with an Avis tag on the front. The driver appeared to be alone. Hardy continued to watch as the car pulled into the tiny cemetery, circled once, then stopped beneath the giant white oak tree. He scanned the area several times for others, but saw no one else.

Twenty minutes passed. The driver got out of the Ford, walked around stretching his legs and looking at his watch. He was a tall, rangy man with a limp. He got back into the car and drove down the narrow entrance road toward the highway.

Hardy dropped the binoculars and spun out from behind the house and headed down the road. Just before the green Ford reached the blacktop, Hardy pulled into its path. The driver of the Ford slammed on his brakes, a surprised look on his face. He got out of the vehicle and limped toward Hardy. Hardy reached over and stuck the .44 down between the seat and the door on his left, readily accessible.

The man came around to the driver's side. Hardy locked the doors and cracked the window.

"*Semper Fi,* Mr. Jackson, I presume? I'm Ben Wasserman. I congratulate you. The Bureau couldn't have done it better. I assure you I'm alone."

"Let me see some ID."

The man reached inside his coat. Hardy's hand moved toward the revolver. He produced a laminated ID. Hardy studied the photo a minute, then the man's face.

"Okay, so you're with the Department of Justice. What do you want?"

"To talk."

"Get in," Hardy said, unlocking the doors.

Ben walked around the car and slid in the front seat. Hardy backed out and drove up the hill and behind the old farmhouse where he had a good view of anyone approaching. He turned in the seat and faced Ben and said, "I'm listening."

"Mr. Jackson, I work for the Office of Special Investigation. Our job is to locate individuals who have entered the country under false pretenses. Primarily, we track down Nazi's who have committed war crimes. I believe the reichsmarks you listed for sale are connected to a case we are currently investigating."

"So what if I did list the reichsmarks? Is that against the law?"

"No, it isn't," said Ben. "But maybe you can tell me why you rented a post office box in the name of Joe Smith and had a man named Doolittle pick up the mail."

"Who says I did?"

"What is really interesting is why Doolittle was killed."

Hardy's insides tightened. Suddenly, he felt warm. He cracked the window.

"But you know something, Mr. Jackson, the most interesting question is why your fingerprints were found in the victim's room."

Hardy twisted in the seat and met Ben's gaze head on. "Look, I haven't killed anyone."

"The Huntsville P.D. hasn't reached that conclusion."

"What are you talking about?"

"Presently, you are their only suspect."

"Then why haven't they arrested me?"

"My office has asked them to hold off."

"Why?"

"I believe you have information that is vital to our investigation. We aren't interested in prosecuting you. We want your cooperation." Ben paused. "As long as you cooperate, I can assure you that the locals will take no legal action against you."

"And what if I don't?"

"You could be charged with murder."

He felt hot—sick. He knew how the legal system worked. Some hotshot assistant DA looking for a chance to jump-start his career would relish trying a lawyer for murder.

"So what if my prints were found in the room? That doesn't prove I murdered him," Hardy said. "You'd have to prove some kind of motive, and what could that have been? Robbery?"

"That's true. It's circumstantial. But taken with a handkerchief with the monogram *J.H.J.* and Doolittle's blood and the circumstances start to pile up, Mr. Jackson."

After a long pause, "How do I know you don't have a wire on you right now? You are a total stranger. Why should I trust you?"

"Because you really don't have any choice," said Wasserman. "You can cooperate with us or deal with the good ol' boys in Huntsville."

"That's not much of an option," replied Hardy. "But I guess I'd rather be at the mercy of the Feds than a bunch of redneck cops in Huntsville."

"Okay, where did you get the reichsmarks?"

"I found them in my father's footlocker after he died. I needed money and I thought they might have some value."

"Why use a false name in renting the post office box?"

"I didn't want to be connected to the reichsmarks."

"Why was Doolittle picking up your mail?"

"Like I said, I didn't want to be connected. But I didn't have anything to do with his death."

"Do you have any idea who might have killed Doolittle?"

Hardy reached in the back seat for a brown leather valise and Wasserman drew back quickly.

"Take it easy," said Hardy. "I got something to show you."

Hardy opened the valise and pulled out a plastic bag containing a cigarette box. "Take a look at this."

"Goulasis," said Wasserman. "Where did you get these?"

"In Doolittle's room."

"Go on."

Hardy recounted everything that had happened, including the blue Chevy that had followed him from the motel. "I can't say for sure that I was being followed, but at the time I thought I was." He didn't mention Millie's death or his encounter with the German at his house.

"What else did you find in the footlocker?"

"Luger, boots, a uniform, Army blanket—stuff like that."

"Have you told me everything?"

"Yeah."

"Very well." Wasserman reached inside his shirt pocket, found a card and scribbled a number on it and gave it to Hardy. "In case you have forgotten to tell me everything, I can be reached at the Huntsville FBI office for the next few days. Now, if you'll drive me back to my car."

Hardy drove back down the road to where the car was parked. Wasserman opened the door and slid out of the car, then turned. "Sooner or later the Huntsville Police will have to take action. I can't hold them at bay forever. And sooner or later, the Nazis will find you, if they haven't already. They are dangerous people. They will kill you without blinking an eye. Don't wait too long to call me, Mr. Jackson."

"Where did you serve with the Corps?" Hardy asked.

"Vietnam."

* * * *

Hardy drove the back roads for a long time, thinking, trying to figure a way out. Perhaps, he should've come clean with Wasserman about the document and the German who broke into his house. They already killed Millie. But, he didn't trust the damn government. He needed time to think. What if Doolittle collapsed days after the day he fell and struck his head. He may have indirectly caused his death when he startled him and he fell. Shit. But that doesn't explain the pack of German cigarettes in his room and the car that followed him. Somehow those had to be connected with the old man's death. He just had to find a way to prove it.

When he reached Beauregard Street, he killed the headlights and circled the block looking for unfamiliar cars. The yellow bulb outside his garage glowed dimly in the night. Everything appeared normal. He circled the block once more and pulled into the garage and lowered the door. He tried to remember where he'd last seen the sleeping bag. Grabbing the revolver, he slid from the car, unlocked the door and entered the house. After checking around downstairs, he bounded up the stairs and went to his son's room. The sleeping bag was in the closet on the top shelf behind some quilts. He grabbed it and found his green down jacket. He went downstairs and was out of the house in seconds.

The blacktop north of town was straight and level for several miles, making it easy to see if someone was following. He doubled back once just to be sure, then headed toward Taylor's cotton gin.

He called Sarah on the cell phone. Her answering machine clicked on.

"Dammit!" He barked. "Sarah, if you're there pick up!"

Then he remembered. Sarah wasn't at her apartment. She and Jasmine had gone to stay with her uncle on his dairy farm in the western part of the county. He got a number from information and called. An old-sounding man answered.

"This is Hardy Jackson. I need to talk to Sarah."

"Say again?" The man yelled at someone. "Somebody turn that dratted TV down." He spoke in the phone again. "Now say what?"

"I said this is Hardy Jackson."

"Oh, hello."

"I need to talk to Sarah. Is she there?" Hardy heard the receiver bang against something and then there was silence for a brief moment before Sarah picked up.

"Hardy, where are you? Are you all right? I've been worried sick."

"I'm fine. What about you and Jasmine?"

She exhaled with relief. "Thank God. And yes, we're fine. The farm is isolated and if any strangers come around, the whole community will know about it."

"Great."

"Where are you?"

"I'm on my way to my hiding place. You know where."

"Did something else happen?"

"Not really," he said.

"What did Wasserman say?"
"I'll tell you later."
"I'm coming up," she said.
"It isn't necessary."
"I don't care," she said. "I'm coming up. Anyway, you'll need something to eat."
"If you do come, drive to the back and blink your lights twice. And Sarah…"
"Yes?"
"Be damn sure you aren't followed."

* * * *

At Taylor's gin he parked the Thunderbird under the tin shed out of view of any passing cars and entered the gin building through an unlocked window. He unrolled the sleeping bag and draped it around his shoulders and waited in the darkness. The revolver was close at his side. He couldn't keep up this nerve-wracking pace much longer. He knew the German would return, probably with reinforcements. The document imperiled his life, yet it was his only insurance. If he handed it over to them, they would kill him for sure. If he told the Feds about it, there was nothing to say they would protect him. They still might feed him to the cops who were looking for someone to hang Doolittle's death on.

Later, he heard a car engine and jumped to his feet, revolver in hand. Lights blinked twice. It was Sarah. He stuffed the revolver inside his belt and unlocked the door and held it open as Sarah ran toward him.

"Har…deee!"
"Yeah."
She rushed into the building, her eyes wide and hands trembling. "Oh God, I've been so worried."
"I'm okay."
"I'm so sorry." Her eyes teared up.
"About what?"
"For every nasty remark I've ever made to you. I didn't mean them. I don't want you to be hurt—or killed. Now tell me what happened."
They stood in the darkness and Hardy told her everything.
"Did you tell him about the document?"
"No, I didn't."
"Why not, for God's sake?"
"It's our only insurance."

"You can't hide out forever," she said. "What are we going to do?"

Hardy shook his head and stared into the darkness for a moment. "I don't know. I'm like a trapped animal."

"Maybe the police will find whoever it was that broke into your house."

"I wouldn't count on it. Anyway, if they do locate the guy, others will just take his place. We've landed in the middle of something that could be monumental, and I don't understand any of it. Between now and morning, I'll figure out something and call you."

"You sure?"

"Yeah, now go, and be careful."

She turned to leave. "Oh, I almost forgot." She reached into the pocket of her parka and handed him a paper sack containing a double cheeseburger. "No mayonnaise, right?"

"Thanks."

Hardy stood in the doorway and watched as she walked to the car. When she opened the door to get in, she turned and called out, "Please be careful."

"Don't worry."

* * * *

Three men in a blue Chevy in the woods across the road from the cotton gin watched the taillights of the Volvo disappear into the night.

"Let's go," the big one said, reaching for the door handle.

"Patience, kamerad. First ve give him time to doze off. From the snoring in the back seat, it sounds as though our young friend has already decided on a nap."

Blucker hated having to depend on these Aryan Brotherhood types. All muscle and no brains. So undisciplined. They had not bled for the Fatherland and the Fuhrer's dream, as he had those long years ago. They were two generations removed from Germany, at best. Most, like the reposing Frederick sprawled in the backseat, loose lips flapping with every exhaled breath, knew only mayhem. Their shaved heads, swastika tattoos, leather. Ach! They made him sick.

Frederick was out of the penitentiary on some legal technicality, but his dossier said that he had been part of a prison-based white supremacist gang charged with racketeering. That's all it was to them, some kind of masquerading Mafia, bound by nothing more than their hatred of blacks and Jews. Why did he have to get stuck with him? Something about him being the part of the American contingent traveling to Germany for April 20. "Trust him," Heinz said. Ach.

Chapter 34

Ben was racing the clock and the clock was winning. The AG's insistence that Sunny Webber's story be corroborated had taken valuable time. Now that he knew Raven's identity, he couldn't find him. His secretary said he had taken a trip, but she didn't know, or wouldn't say, where he had gone. Just an hour earlier, they'd visited his home. No one was there. They were checking airlines, but hard information was slow in coming. No doubt Raven had used an assumed name. Certainly, he had forged documents. And the very best.

Ben set his coffee on the desk next to a half-eaten pizza—his third cup since midnight—and loosened his tie and collar. He did a few head rolls and massaged the back of his neck.

Preston burst through the door, looking grim, a file folder in his hand.

"On a hunch, I rousted the court clerk at his home and we went down to the courthouse and did an online search." Preston dropped the file on top of the cold pizza.

Ben studied Preston's face which cracked into a grin. He snatched up the file and fingered through the documents—a divorce complaint, answer and interrogatories. He perused the complaint, quickly moving to the last page and the signature at the bottom. It was signed by Hardy Jackson. He grabbed the phone, got information and obtained the office and home number of Jackson, then called. No answer.

"What's her name?" Ben mumbled and tapped his forehead with a finger. His memory failed him.

"Who?" asked Preston.

"Jackson's law partner."

"Dunnavant?"

Ben snapped his fingers. "That's it! Sarah Dickerson-Dunnavant."

He obtained her number from information and called. As the phone rang at the other end, he reached in his pocket and removed his father's watch and checked the time. It was 1 a.m. The phone rang, but no one answered. After a call to the French Springs PD, he soon had the name and number of Jackson's secretary, Tommye Ann Green. He called her and a sleepy voice answered on the fifth ring.

"Hello?"

"Ms. Green, this is Ben Wasserman with the Department of Justice."

"Yeah, and this is the White House. You've got some nerve."

"Please don't hang up. I'm dead serious. I apologize for calling at such an ungodly hour, but it's very important that I speak to Mr. Jackson immediately."

"Well, he ain't here," she said. "Look, mister, I wasn't born yesterday. I'm not about to give out that information to someone who calls me up in the middle of the night."

"What about Ms. Dunnavant?" he asked. "Do you know where she is?"

"No, and I wouldn't tell you if I knew that either. Now leave me alone."

"No wait! It is imperative that I speak with Mr. Jackson or Ms. Dunnavant on a matter of national security. If I have to send the FBI over to bring you to Huntsville, I will."

"Are you the fella that was at the office yesterday afternoon?"

"Yes."

"If I help you out, do you promise you won't tell how you found out?"

"Sure," said Ben.

"I don't know where Hardy is, but you can reach Sarah at this number." Ben jotted it down.

"Thank you." Ben disconnected, and then called the number. Someone answered on the fourth ring.

"Hallo?" said an elderly man. Ben identified himself and explained his mission.

"Say agin. My hearing ain't too good these days."

Ben repeated himself, louder this time.

"Jest a minute. I'll have to find my britches and go wake 'er" The phone banged on the table and Ben could hear the old man moving about.

In a few minutes a woman's voice said, "Hello?"

"Ms. Dunnavant?"

"Who is this?"

"This is Ben Wasserman with OSI. I apologize for…"
"How did you locate me?"
"With great difficulty."
"Do you know what time it is?"
"It's imperative that I speak with Mr. Jackson immediately. Do you know where I can find him?"
"Why? What for?"
"Does he represent a Sylvia Birch?"
"Yes. We both do."
Ben stood, excited. "Do you know where I can locate her?"
"At her apartment in Huntsville, I suppose."
"Great! What's her phone number?"
"It's in the file at the office," she said. "Say, what's all this about?"
"Where is Mr. Jackson?"
"Why do you want to know?"
"His life may be in great danger."
"No!" she gasped. "Not again. What happened?"
"There isn't time to explain. Please tell me where he is."
There was long silence before she spoke. "Give me time to dress and meet me in front of my office."
"I'll be there in thirty minutes," Ben said, slamming down the phone. He grabbed the file and his coat and headed for the door.
"What's up?" Preston shouted.
"Keep checking the airlines. Try the name Sylvia Birch. I'll be in touch."

* * * *

Hardy sat on a pile of loose cotton with the sleeping bag draped around him and stared into the darkness. If someone came looking for him, he needed a plan of action. The building was tall and rectangular with a catwalk that spanned the ceiling. Facing him were four large ginning machines bolted to the concrete floor. They were powered by dozens of unguarded belts, pulleys and flywheels. When the gins were operating, it was a dangerous place. He peered into the darkness until his eyes ached and the objects faded to a blur. Finally, so exhausted he could no longer hold his eyes open, he lay back on the soft cotton. And he slept.

He woke from a deep sleep and sat upright. A noise. What was it? A squirrel or bird inside the building? No. He heard it again. The unmistakable creak of shoe leather. It had come from his right. He strained to see in the darkness. He heard heavy breathing. He rolled over and grabbed for the pistol. A blinding light struck him in the face and excruciating pain shot up his right arm as a foot ground into his hand.

"You are much too slow," said a thick, accented voice. Not the same one from that night in his darkened house. A jarring blow caught him across the face. A bright light exploded before darkness closed in. Afterwards, as consciousness returned, along with pain, he tasted blood.

"Ver is the document? Tell me before I kill you."

Dazed, Hardy looked up through a blinding light to three hulking black silhouettes crouching over him. The speaker was huge with meaty arms and mallet size hands. One held a revolver on him while another one moved menacingly toward his other side.

"Tell me, ver is the document?" The big one lifted his foot off Hardy's right hand, grabbed it and bent back his little finger. The one with the gun stuck it to Hardy's temple and said, "Now tell us!"

Before Hardy could open his mouth, the brute pushed back his finger snapping the bone.

"Oh God! Please." Pain shot up Hardy's arm and spread throughout his body making him ill. He gagged and fought back the bile in his throat.

"Now, vill you tell me?" The brute grabbed Hardy's ring finger and bent it back.

"Yes, yes! No more, please."

"And no tricks this time, Herr Jackson," said a familiar voice coming from the one holding the flashlight and revolver.

"It's hidden...up there," Hardy said looking up toward the catwalk.

"Ver is the light switch?"

"Near the door."

"Show us."

The brute jerked Hardy to his feet. He reeled from pain but managed to steady himself and cradle his throbbing right hand. He led the men toward the door where the main switch box was located. Maybe he could jerk open the door and escape into the night before they got off some rounds. Maybe. But he didn't know if the door was locked. Once the lights were turned on, he knew his chance of escaping would be slim. It was now or never. The lever that activated power to the cotton gins was beside the switch box. He'd seen old man Taylor start the gin many times. Nearby was the light switch.

When they reached the panel, Hardy said, "I'll need some light to figure this out."

The man holding the flashlight pointed the beam at the controls on the wall. Hardy threw the breaker switch on the big box, then flipped another switch. Fluorescent flickered blinked on. For a fleeting second he saw his captors. The big one was bull necked and bald. Another wore a black eye patch on his ugly, scarred face. And a younger one, looking like some biker, just grinned, showing large, yellowed, gold-capped teeth, a trickle of tobacco juice seeping from the corner of his mouth. Hardy reached over and pulled another lever and the gin roared into gear with a tremendous noise. The trio of intruders started as their eyes swung to the noisy machinery. Hardy flicked off the overhead lights and bolted into the dark labyrinth of roaring belts, pulleys and flywheels.

"Hey, asshole, you trying to make this a game or what? That's O.K., pretty-boy lawyer, I'm up for it!"

Hardy was startled to hear the American accent, but he continued on toward a low window on the opposite side of the building where old man Taylor used to sit and look outside while he ginned. If only he could wriggle his way through the maze of machinery and belts before the Germans found the light switch. The window was his only hope. The lights came on. He dropped to the concrete floor on his left, holding his injured hand, and scooted behind a large spinning pulley.

"Ver is he?"

He breathed a sigh of relief and peered around the pulley and saw a pair of legs coming toward him. It was the one with the eye patch, but where was the big one? The window wasn't more than twenty feet away. He scrambled to his feet and bolted toward the window. A blow to the face sent him crashing to the concrete floor on his back. His head popped against the concrete and consciousness faded. Suddenly, he was jerked to his feet. The old brute on one side and the foul-smelling American on the other dragged him over toward one of the gin heads.

"Now, you vill talk." The brute lifted the safety panel covering the spinning metal saws that separated lint from cottonseeds.

"Don't kill him, Heinz!" yelled the German with the eye patch.

"Don't vorry, kamerad, I vill only show him a little pain. Then he vill talk."

"I hope he don't talk—real soon, anyway," snickered the American.

"Enough!" said the German with the eye patch. "Ve have a job to do. This is not a game."

The brute grabbed Hardy's left hand and pulled it down toward the spinning saw blades. He fought back, but the German's young assistant added his strength and Hardy was no match. He knew what the saws could do to a man's arm. He made a quick stabbing motion with his injured right hand and two fingers found their mark, poking deep into the old brute's eye sockets. He screamed, grabbed for his eyes, turned sharply in the direction of the American, and in so doing, loosened his grip on Hardy's arm. The American stumbled backward and fell, but soon regained his footing and charged toward Hardy with a determined growl. But in one motion Hardy spun, and with a sharp snap, landed a heel in the old man's spongy groin. The brute groaned and doubled forward. Hardy grabbed his arm and swung the heavily-muscled, but overweight body into the oncoming American.

"Oof!," the younger gasped as the German landed against his midsection, knocking the wind out of him and sending them both sprawling. Hardy bent and grasped the German, hauling him up and heaving his hand into the spinning gin saws. His scream was ear piercing, even above the roar of the machinery.

The metal blades chewed in and slung blood and tissue against metal, drawing his macerated arm ever deeper into the gin. Gore slung far and splattered the American's face and he made swiping motions at his eyes.

Hardy whirled around, remembering the other old German. He saw him silhouetted against the moonlight streaming in through the window as he wove his way through the belts and pulleys, not toward him, but toward the low window. The machinery ground to a halt as someone cut the power. The startled American ran in the direction of the retreating German.

Hardy looked toward the entrance in the sudden echoing silence and saw a man and woman coming. Wasserman and Sarah. Thank God.

The German with the eye patch crashed through the window, shoved unceremoniously by the scrambling American, and the pair kept going, escaping into the darkness with Wasserman in pursuit, firing at the fleeing assailants. The brute, his arm shredded to the shoulder, lay draped across the gin heads. Hardy clasped his injured hand.

✯   ✯   ✯   ✯

Sarah splinted Hardy's broken finger with a ball point pen, binding it with a handkerchief. A winded Wasserman came stumbling in to the gin.

"I lost them," he panted. "They were across the road and into their car before I got as far as the road. They damn near ran me down."

Wasserman walked over and nudged the dead German and the corpulent body slid to the floor in a bloody heap. He looked with palpable disgust at the soiled toe of this well-shined shoe. He bent and wiped his shoe with a clean handkerchief and flung the soiled linen into the machinery before coming to examine Hardy's mouth. "A loose tooth and cuts, but you'll live."

"What about my jaw? It feels broken," Hardy said, barely able to open his mouth.

Wasserman worked Hardy's jaw up and down a few times. "Not broken. Come on, let's get you to the ER. I'll call for someone to clean up here."

Hardy insisted they take his T-Bird to French Springs. Wasserman looked into the rearview mirror at Hardy sitting in the back seat cradling his jaw with his good hand. "Now, Mr. Jackson are you ready to cooperate?"

"For Pete's sake, tell him everything," Sarah pleaded.

Hardy, his jaw throbbing with pain, nodded his head.

"Do you know where Sylvia Birch is?" Wasserman asked.

Hardy shook his head.

Sarah said, "The last we heard, she and her husband had reconciled."

"Tell him everything, Sarah," Hardy mumbled, barely moving his jaw.

Sarah told him about the document and the late-night attack on Hardy in his house.

"Where is it?" asked Wasserman.

"How do I know you still won't try to hang Doolittle's death on me.?"

Wasserman braked and pulled onto the shoulder.

"Forget that for now! Can't you see there is more at stake? These monsters killed your wife and nearly killed you and they'll not stop. The stakes are too high. Good God, man, we need you to cooperate now. Jackson, there are times in life when we're called upon to stand up for what's right. This is one of those times.

"My father, like you, was a lawyer. He practiced in Berlin. He busied himself with the law and left politics to the politicians. When the Nazi brown shirts marched in the streets and made their threats, he wasn't concerned. After all, there were only a few of them. When they came to power in 1933, production surged and employment expanded. People were working. They were bloated with contentment. They didn't pay much attention when opposition politicians were carted off to concentration camps. Nor when homosexuals and artists were locked up. My father heard rumors of Jews being sent to camps, but he wasn't unduly concerned. He was a prominent attorney. That kind of thing couldn't happen to him, he thought. The day the trucks came to our apartment, my mother and I were visiting in the countryside. We escaped Germany. My father died in Auschwitz" He paused. "What I'm saying, Jackson, is that good people can't afford to sit idly by."

Wasserman's cell phone buzzed. "This is Ben," he snapped into the phone. "I'm on my way back to French Springs. Any new information? Great! That's great. Good work." He replaced the phone and twisted his head around and toward Hardy, "We've located your client. She and a male companion departed Atlanta last night on a flight to Munich."

He paused. "We believe her life to be in grave danger."

"Why?" asked Sarah.

"I can't reveal that information. I can only tell you that there are forces at work that would stop at nothing to achieve their ends."

"And what's that?" Hardy asked.

"Jackson, it is imperative that I locate Sylvia Birch immediately."

Hardy thought of the big-eyed beauty in his office who bitterly wept out the tale of her husband's infidelity. And then the memory of Millie's bloodied, lifeless face under the glare of ER lights swam before Hardy's eyes. He didn't know how Sylvia Birch figured into this mess, but another innocent woman must not die. He would make whoever killed his gentle wife pay before they could harm anyone else. "I can help you find her. She knows me."

Ben glanced in the mirror at Hardy. "You're a civilian. This is too dangerous. You can be of the most help to us by just handing over the document."

"Not unless you take me with you to Sylvia Birch," Hardy insisted.

"I can't even get security clearance for you. This is that sensitive. We need that document now, Jackson. That is the part you can do. When the world was threatened by Nazism, your father picked up arms and helped destroy it. He did it for his unborn son. He sacrificed so that you could live in peace. Now the world is again threatened. You have a son, Jackson. Will you act to make the world safe for him as your father did for you? Or will you sit back and do nothing and let someone else fight your battle?"

"It's imperative that I go," Hardy said. "All you have to go on is the sound of his voice. But I can get close to Sylvia Birch. She is in danger. I can get close to her and talk her away from her husband. She has never laid eyes on you. She won't trust you or believe what you have to say. She loves her husband. But she knows me. If anyone can get to her, I can."

Ben listened in silence, then reluctantly jerked his head. "Okay. But Jackson, there's a good chance none of us will come out of this alive."

Hardy struggled with the door latch, got out and popped the left front hubcap, removed a tightly folded paper and handed it to Wasserman.

Wasserman stood in front of the headlight and read. He glanced up at Hardy. "Jesus Christ. No wonder they are after you. Get in the car."

* * * *

Hardy's right hand and jaw were X-rayed at the ER, his finger splinted and he was given something for his pain. Ben left for Huntsville, saying he would ask that an all-points bulletin be put out for the German and American who escaped and notify authorities of the dead one at the cotton gin.

Afterward, Hardy and Sarah drove to her Uncle's farm.

Sarah pulled out the couch, smoothed on sheets and brought in extra quilts.

"If you need anything I'll be down the hallway, second door on the left."

Hardy reached over and pulled her to his chest. "Thank you."

"What are we going to do," she asked looking up at him.

"I'll think of something."

"We can't hide forever."

"I know." He kissed her on the forehead. "Now go to bed."

Hardy turned off the lamp and sat on the edge of the unfolded couch and stared into the darkness. He couldn't sleep. His finger throbbed. He found the pain pills the ER physician had given him and took another one. But Wasserman's words echoed in his mind. The truth was that he had had it easy all of his life. His parents survived the Great Depression and fought against tyranny. The worst thing he had to put up with was practicing law before The Warthog.

He walked over to the window and stood in his shorts looking out at rolling hills barely visible in the dim moonlight. The Nazi bastard had run Millie off the road and killed her then tried to kill him. Millie was gone. What did he have to live for but finding and killing them all?

* * * *

It was 5:30 a.m., Washington time, when Wasserman, calling from a secure FBI phone, reached the attorney general in her Georgetown apartment. She was asleep.

"General, I apologize for calling at this early hour, but I have news."

"Let's hear it."

"Wolfgang Hitler has been identified!"

"Are you sure you have the right man?"

"Positive."

"Where is he now?"

"He departed Atlanta yesterday with his wife on Lufthansa bound for Munich."

"What time?"

"1:30 Eastern."

"Let's see…they would arrive at…"

"9:30."

"Is the woman involved?" she asked.

"No. In fact, she recently filed for divorce. That could have blown his cover. I suspect he has lured her to Germany to have her killed."

"And General, there is one other bizarre fact that has emerged."

"What's that?"

"This attorney, Jackson, had possession of what appears to be a power of attorney to Hitler's Swiss bank account."

"Is it authentic?"

"The crime lab is checking it out."

"That's incredible."

"Somehow the Raven Group learned of its whereabouts and came after it. They killed an old man and Jackson's wife and one of the Raven Group is dead. Two others escaped."

"Intelligence indicates a large gathering of Neo-Nazis in Munich," she said. "I'm told that every hotel room has been booked for April 19. Hitler began his rise to power in Munich. What better city is there for his heir apparent to make his grand entrance? We must find him and stop him before he appears."

"It may be too late," Ben said.

"Find him, Ben!"

"And if I do?"

"Go to the nearest American embassy or consulate and notify me immediately. You'll have backup in the area. Someone else will take over from that point."

Chapter 35

The black Mercedes sped down the Autobahn southeast of Munich through the rolling Bavarian countryside. Rudy, nattily dressed in a brown turtleneck sweater and matching sport coat, took one hand off the wheel to stroke Sylvia's thigh.

"Darling, I promise this will be a memorable trip."

Sylvia stared intently into her husband's eyes, searching for any hint of insincerity.

"I need to ask you something." Her tone was serious.

"Certainly, darling."

She hesitated, "Why, is there a recording device on our phone?"

Rudy's head snapped toward her, then back to the road. He was silent for a moment. "Oh that," he said lightly.

"I want to know."

"It's embarrassing to admit, but I was jealous. I thought you were seeing someone when I was out of town."

Sylvia studied her husband's face. "Really?"

"Yeah, really."

She managed a smile, then said, "And I thought I was the jealous one." After a moment of reflection, she said, "Yes, I'm looking forward to our time together."

"We should have done this long ago."

"Where are we going?"

"The most beautiful spot in the Austrian Alps."

They crossed into Austria and west of Salzburg turned south onto a two-lane road that wound through rugged mountains. Twilight was gathering when they entered a long, snow-covered valley. The lights of a town twinkled in the distance.

"Well, here we are, darling," Rudy said. "Kitzbuhel. You'll love it."

They drove down a bumpy cobblestone street, turned onto Alfons-Pitzold-Weg and pulled in at the Alpen Haus. It was a quaint three-story stucco with smoke rising from the chimney. Hemingwayesque, Sylvia thought.

Rudy parked, came around and opened Sylvia's door, and took her hand to lead her across the snow. She shivered in the coldness and Rudy pulled her close under his arm. In the small, dimly lighted lobby, a heavyset woman with dark eyes, gray hair and a mouth that turned down, greeted them with a thick accent. "Herr Birch, velcome to Kitzbuhel. I have been expecting you."

Rudy smiled. "Frau Schradmann, I would like for you to meet my wife, Sylvia."

The older woman curtseyed and shook Sylvia's hand very formally.

"Velcome, Frau Birch. I hope you vill enjoy your holiday. I know you are tired. Come, let me show you to your room."

Frau Schradmann looked over at a man sitting by a tile wood-burning stove. He was large with big arms and a thick neck.

"Hansel, vill you bring in our guests' luggage?"

Frau Schradmann escorted them up a wooden staircase, its white walls hung with ornately framed oil landscapes. On the third floor, she ushered them into a small but elegant room. She walked over to a large window and threw back the drapes.

"Tomorrow morning you vill have a grand view of the Alps. Now rest. Dinner is served at seven."

After Frau Schradmann departed, Rudy took Sylvia's hand and lead her to the window overlooking the town. Snow had begun to fall. Big flakes, the size of nickels floated lazily down. Somewhere in the distance, she thought she heard Mozart. Her suspicions of Rudy and misgivings about the trip seemed to vanish. She did love her husband so. Her love, so crushed by his infidelity, now came back stronger than ever. "Oh, sweetheart, it's so beautiful. Thank you for bringing me here." She leaned into him and he enclosed her in his strong arms. "I love you," she whispered against his neck.

"And I love you."

"Rudy…I have a wonderful idea on how we can seal our love. And I think this trip might be the perfect time to get started."

"Oh?"

"A child," she stated simply. "It's not too late for me. I want this experience. I want it to be with you."

*   *   *   *

Under the down-filled duvet, Rudy explored the dark recesses of Sylvia's open body as she strained against him, gasping his name over and over.

"You're not wearing your diaphragm!" he said.

"I left it at home," she whispered meekly.

"You and your romantic ideas."

"I'm in charge this time," she murmured as the tip of her tongue wound through the tightly curling mass on his chest.

Oh, well. What did it really matter?

Chapter 36

The Lufthansa 747 lumbered down Atlanta-Hartsfield runway and lifted into the gray haze. Hardy closed his eyes and said a silent prayer. When he heard the landing gear retract, he opened his eyes and saw day fading into night on the horizon.

"I need a drink," he said to Ben, seated beside him looking pensive.

"Excellent idea."

Shortly, two blonde hostesses appeared in the aisle pushing a serving tray and taking drink orders. Hardy ordered a double Jack Daniels on the rocks and washed down two pain pills. Ben selected a Heineken. Later, the aroma of hot food wafted through the cabin, but he wasn't hungry. Sleep came quickly.

Hardy was hung over when they touched down at Franz Joseph Strauss Airport in Munich the next morning, but otherwise much improved. The swelling in his jaw had subsided and his hand had stopped throbbing. He'd feel a lot better if he could have gotten clearance to bring his .44. Somehow, Ben's gun did not reassure him.

Inside the busy terminal, Ben made a call while Hardy stood nearby. Ben spoke in a lowered voice and wrote something in the palm of his hand. He replaced the receiver. "We're in luck. Sylvia Birch and her husband arrived yesterday. Intelligence sources report they rented a black Mercedes and registered at a pension in Kitzbuhel, Austria."

Ben rented a gray Ford and soon they were barreling southeast down the Autobahn. He handed Hardy a map. "You navigate."

Hardy found Kitzbuhel on the map, calculated the kilometers and converted them to miles. "It's about a hundred miles."

Ben stomped the accelerator and moved over to the fast lane. They rode in silence for a long time.

*   *   *   *

It was just past noon under a bright blue sky when Sylvia and Rudy racked their skis and poles and boarded a cable car to the summit of Kitzbuheler Horn. The car jerked forward on groaning steel cables. Sylvia's heart raced. Embarrassed to say anything lest her voice betray her fear, she grabbed Rudy's hand and squeezed it. The cable car moved slowly up the mountain, swinging in the wind. She closed her eyes and prayed silently.

"Look, darling," Rudy said.

She opened her eyes slowly. Rudy pointed to the jagged snow capped peaks.

"Isn't it beautiful?" he said.

At the summit, the gondola stopped inside a concrete building where giant metal cogs and wheels wound the cables. They got off, got their poles and skis from the rack, and walked onto the glistening snow. Colorfully clad skiers shot off down the mountain. Rudy located an uncrowded area where the slope was gradual and announced it would be an excellent place to begin lessons. First, he showed her how to snap into her skis and how to hold her poles. Then he showed her how to snowplow. He demonstrated the technique.

"See, when you want to stop, just point the tips of your skis together, like this."

It looked easy enough. She pushed off cautiously with her poles and moved forward, uncertain and wobbly at first.

"Bend you knees and lean forward a little more," he said.

She did and moved down the gentle slope. It was easy! Her confidence soared. After a short distance, she pointed the tips of her skis together and plowed to a stop.

Rudy skied up beside her. "Excellent! Darling, you are a natural."

Next, he taught her how to make turns. "Remember, if you want to turn left, press down on your right ski, and vice versa. Okay?"

Sylvia nodded her head and pushed off down a long, broad slope bordered by trees.

"Practice your turns," Rudy yelled.

She pressed down on her right ski and made a slow left turn. When she neared the forest edge on the other side of the run, she pressed on her left ski and turned right. It was easy. She continued down the mountain, making slow broad turns with Rudy behind her offering encouragement and advice.

"Now, pull your skis closer together and pick up your speed," he said.

She did as he had instructed and immediately her speed increased. She shot off down the mountain so quickly that it frightened her.

"Turn! It will slow you," Rudy yelled.

She panicked. Which ski was she to press? Left or right? She couldn't remember. Looking up, she saw trees rushing toward her. She brought the tip of her skis together and tried to snowplow, but in her haste, she overcorrected. The skis crossed.

"Sit down!" Rudy yelled. But it was too late. She was already airborne. Skis spun over her head like helicopter blades. She landed hard and her face plowed up snow. She squeezed her eyes shut. "Oh, no!" Something hard against her arm brought her ignoble slide to a sudden stop. She opened her eyes and looked around. She was stuck in deep powder and was hugging a small tree. Otherwise, she was fine.

Rudy skied up. "Darling, are you okay?"

She blew snow out of her nostrils before answering. "Get me out of this."

"He laughed and pulled her out of the powder. He brushed the snow from her outfit, lingering for an added swipe at her rounded bottom, but she was in no mood for his playfulness.

"I've had enough," she announced emphatically.

"When a horse throws you, you must get back on. I'll help you." She snapped back in her skis and searched for her sunglasses. Rudy found them in the snow, smashed.

"Let's take a break. Follow me," he said. They skied to a spot that offered a panoramic view of the valley. He popped out of his skis and helped Sylvia do the same and stuck them and the poles upright in the snow. Shrugging off his backpack, he lifted out a bottle of Mosel Kabinet and a loaf of French bread. He uncorked the wine and poured it in plastic cups. "To the good life."

"To the good life," Sylvia replied flatly.

They drank. Rudy broke off chunks of fresh bread and they ate and drank the wine. The sun warmed her face, good bread and good wine warmed her stomach, and she started to thaw toward the man who had gotten her into this uncomfortable adventure. The cold air tingling her skin and the wine warming her insides, Sylvia felt totally alive. Other husbands cheated, wives found out, and they put it behind them and the marriages went on.

* * * *

Ben turned onto Alfons-Pitzold-Weg and drove slowly down the snow-banked street checking out cars. They had driven only a short distance when Hardy spotted a black car in the driveway of a pension. "I think I see it!"

Hardy pointed toward a Mercedes partially covered with fresh snow.

"Can you see the tag number?"

Hardy rolled down the window and shaded his eyes with a hand.

"Bingo!"

"Let's leave before we're seen," Ben said.

Hardy glanced toward the pension and saw a window curtain part. "It's too late." He gestured with his head toward a window where a half face peered through slitted curtains.

"Let's go," said Ben.

They drove down the street, turned around and headed back toward the center of town. Ben pulled to the curb near a sidewalk cafe. "Wait while I use the phone."

Hardy waited in the car, wishing he had his revolver.

* * * *

After they finished the bread and wine, Rudy stood and brushed the snow from his clothes. "Come, I want to show you a magnificent place."

"Can't we stay here? I'm tired."

"No, darling, you are only afraid."

"Yes, I suppose you're right."

He reached down and took her hand and helped her to her feet. They snapped into their skis. Sylvia was giddy and unstable on her feet.

"I think I'm drunk," she giggled.

Rudy pushed off and glided quickly down the mountain, Sylvia close behind. The alcohol gave her false confidence. The only sound was the swish of skis cutting through powder. Rudy was right, fear robs joy from life. She skied several hundred feet behind Rudy. The sun was bright against the snow and without her shades it was difficult to judge distances. Rudy veered off to the right, away from other skiers, toward the edge of the mountain. She heard a skier coming up behind her. She glanced over her shoulder.

It was a large man with big arms and shoulders in a black ski mask. He looked familiar. And he was only a few feet behind her. She brought her skis closer together and picked up speed. She looked back again. The man was still on her tail.

"Back off!" she yelled. "Ruuudy!"

"Over here, darling."

She turned toward his voice. Now the man would stop coming on to her. The snow was blinding. She panicked. What had Rudy said about stopping? Snowplow. Yes, that was it. She felt a hand on her back and looked around. It was him, the large man in the black mask.

"I vill help you," he said.

Now she recognized him. It was Hansel from the Alpen Haus and he was pushing her. "No! Leave me alone! Look, I don't need your help. Stop it!" She swung at him with a ski pole. He grabbed both of her shoulders and guided her toward Rudy's voice. She tried to wriggle loose, but she couldn't shake his iron grip.

She looked around for Rudy and saw him standing calmly near a sign with large red letters: "Verboten." Why didn't Rudy help? Hansel guided her toward the sign. She saw Kitzbuhel far below. Rudy continued to gaze at her in a placid, unconcerned manner. Just then, Hansel gave her a hard push.

The updraft took her breath away and stole the scream that split her terrorized mind. She sailed over the edge, falling facedown, flailing at the cold, blue sky with ski poles still looped to her hands. *This can't be happening. I'm not ready to die. Why didn't Rudy help me?* Her mind raced as she plummeted toward earth. Wind rushed past her ears. She saw a pile of snow-covered boulders like down-filled pillows awaiting her weary head. Yes. Yes, to rest.

Rudy flinched as Sylvia's body smashed like a rag doll onto the boulders. He turned to Hansel with a queer look almost like regret.

"Poor Sylvia. Did you know, Hansel, that she wanted to bear my child? It could have been, I suppose, a child for the Fatherland. But, *ach,* her bloodlines were all wrong. Come, there is work we must do."

"*Ja.*"

*   *   *   *

Hardy first saw the crowd gathered at the base of the Kitzbuheler Horn, then he saw the ambulance with back doors standing open. Ben saw it too. He pulled over and they walked toward the crowd. Hardy strained to peer above the onlookers and saw the attendants removing a sheet-wrapped body from a ski patrol sled and place it on a gurney.

"What happened?" he asked a bystander.

"Some woman skied off the mountain."

The medics transferred the figure to the gurney, just as a gust of wind flipped the sheet open and Hardy saw the face. Sylvia Birch! He looked up and spied the man in the photo that Sylvia had shown him. Rudy Birch, and seemingly not at all distressed. For an instant their eyes met. "That's him," he whispered to Ben.

"Who?"

"Rudolph Birch."

"Are you certain?"

"Positive."

A big, bull-necked man walked beside Rudy and whispered in his ear. Hardy was speechless, unable to believe what he saw. It was the same brute he had shoved into the cotton gin. How could this be?

"Let's go," Ben said. They got in the car. "You look like you just saw a ghost."

"The bastard I stuck in the cotton gin is still alive, or he has a twin brother. Did you see him?"

"I wasn't paying attention. Here," he handed a map to Hardy. "Which road to Salzburg?"

After studying the map a moment, Hardy said, "Stay on Highway 61. When we get to the 'Y', go right. It looks like it's about 80 kilometers."

"Keep a lookout behind us."

"Why Salzburg?" Hardy asked.

"To use a secure phone at the American Consulate."

✱   ✱   ✱   ✱

It was dark when Ben and Hardy returned to Kitzbuhel from Salzburg. They found a room at a small pension just up the street from the Alpen Haus. It was on the second floor with a window that offered a good view of the black Mercedes.

Ben pulled a chair to the window, cracked the drapes and sat down. "We'll take turns," he said. "You get some sleep while I take first watch."

Chapter 37

It was mid-afternoon, clear and sunny when Hardy rubbed his tired eyes, yawned and got up from his post at the window and went into the bathroom. Ben was lying on the bed in his black wingtips, snoring. Hardy washed his hands and splashed water on his face. He worked his mouth open and shut several times. The soreness in his jaw was almost gone. But his little finger, immobilized in a splint, still hurt.

The thought of Sylvia Birch's broken body made him sick. It was goddamn time Ben let him in on what was going on. It was too late for Sylvia, but he still had a score to settle with these sons of bitches and he had a right to know the whole story.

After drying his face he walked back into the room and over to the window, cracked the drapes and looked toward the Alpen Haus. Someone was coming out. He strained to see clearer. It was the big bull-necked brute. He was carrying a suitcase.

"Wasserman!"

Ben sat up on the side of the bed. "That was a short three hours," he said yawning.

Hardy peered through the sheer draperies. Rudy came out of the Alpen Haus and climbed into the Mercedes.

"They're leaving!" Hardy cried.

Ben rushed to the window. The Mercedes was backing out into the snow-banked street. "Let's go!" he said, grabbing his coat and heading for the door.

Hardy was right on his heels. They took the wooden steps three and four at a time, rushed out the door and ran toward the Ford, which was backed into a parking space. Ben slid behind the wheel and fumbled for the key.

"Watch where they go!" he said.

Hardy twisted around in the seat, craning his neck. "Hurry!"

The Ford's motor turned over and Ben spun out of the parking lot, fishtailing on the compacted snow, meanwhile fishing out his cell phone.

"I see them," Hardy said. "They're turning left at the second intersection."

They were soon on the main road leading north out of Kitzbuhel, staying well behind the Mercedes as Ben punched in numbers and called for reinforcements. Where the highway came to a 'Y', the Mercedes went right and headed northeast on road 312, toward Salzburg.

The black Mercedes was fading in the distance. Ben pressed the pedal and said, "Hang on and pray to God we don't hit ice."

Hardy had a death grip on the dash with his good hand while keeping his eyes trained on the Mercedes, which was growing smaller by the minute.

"What if they see us?" he said.

"We're too far behind."

Hardy felt naked without his revolver. "Do you have an extra weapon?"

Ben's jaw was rigid. "No, why?"

"I don't want to be the dog that caught the car, if you know what I mean."

"Don't worry, we won't," Ben said.

"Don't you think it's about time you leveled with me?"

Ben glanced at Hardy from the corner of his eyes, "I can't."

"If you want to follow that Mercedes you will!" Hardy grasped the ignition key.

"You wouldn't."

"Try me!"

"No, don't!"

"Who the hell is Rudy Birch?"

"A Neo-Nazi."

"Yeah, I already figured that out," Hardy said. "But why are the Feds after him?"

"You don't really want to know."

"Yes, I do."

"It's information that could endanger your life."

"Well, now that's rich," Hardy said. "We're chasing a couple of Neo-fucking-Nazis, and if we catch them we've got one gun between us, and you're worried about endangering my life?"

Ben sighed. "Rudy Birch's real name is Wolfgang Hitler. He's the son of Adolf Hitler and Eva Braun."

"What?"

"Tomorrow is April 20—Adolf Hitler's birthday. His heir is set to make his triumphant return at a large Nazi rally tomorrow in Munich."

Hardy fell back against the seat, his mind reeling. Finally, he looked over at Ben, staring straight ahead. "What if Rudy—uh Wolfgang—isn't stopped?"

"Our government will never permit Wolfgang to reach Munich. The call I made in Salzburg was to our area operatives. We were to meet just this side of Munich for the takedown, but the schedule got moved up some with our subjects' early departure. They're on their way here. We just have to keep phoning our coordinates and hope they make it on time."

They were in a mountainous country and the road was slick with patches of compacted snow. They rounded a curve and saw the brake lights on the Mercedes. The right directional signal flashed on. Ben slowed. The Mercedes turned right on Highway 305 and headed east. Ben swung right and followed. "Look at the map and see where 305 goes."

Hardy studied the map a moment. "Berchtesgaden."

* * * *

Heinz glanced in the rearview mirror. His jaw tightened.

"What is it?" Wolfgang asked.

"I think we have company."

"Are you sure?"

"A gray Ford has been behind us for a long time."

"Lose it," Wolfgang said looking at his watch. "And be quick about it. We don't have much time."

"Ja. There is one way to know if the car is following us." He turned right, crossed a short bridge spanning a narrow river, and headed up the winding mountain road. When he saw the gray Ford turn and follow, he reached across to the glove compartment, removed a P.38 and stuffed it in his belt.

* * * *

Ben was silent ever since they had turned onto the mountain road that led to Obersalzberg.

"What's wrong?" Hardy asked.

"Do you know where this road leads?"

"No. Should I?"

"Hitler's Eagle's Nest."

Hardy swallowed hard and looked around in silence.

"Your father's regiment was here in May 1945," Ben said.

"I didn't know that."

"It was in the dossier."

The narrow road wound through forest. Perhaps Jabo had traveled up this very road. He would have been just a kid.

Ben maneuvered around patches of compacted snow. A granite wall, where the roadway had been cut into the side of the mountain was only a few feet on their right side; a sharp wooded drop-off was on the left. When they neared the top, Hardy looked out to his left, and far below, saw Berchtesgaden.

"I don't like this," Ben growled.

Hardy snapped his head toward Ben.

"The road is dangerous. I have a bad feeling."

The words had barely left Ben's mouth when Hardy saw it. It happened quickly. He grabbed the dash with both hands. "Watch out!"

"They're going to ram us!"

The black Mercedes was speeding straight at the Ford. Ben whipped to the right, but there was no escape. The granite wall blocked them. The heavy Mercedes bore down on them, so close that Hardy saw the two men in the car. Wolfgang was in the front passenger seat. The brute was driving, a grotesque smirk on his ugly face.

Ben cut the steering wheel hard left just as the Mercedes slammed the right rear quarter panel of the Ford. The front of the Ford spun to the right toward the granite wall. Ben wrestled the wheel to the left. The car glanced against the granite, spun back around and was suddenly airborne. For a flickering moment, Hardy saw the Mercedes fishtailing down the road until his vision was obscured by treetops flying past his window. Far below, he saw the beautiful green valley, serene and dream like. The car seemed to float in mid-air for a long time. He thought of Millie, Clint, his mom and of Jabo and then after the wrenching crash he thought no more.

Chapter 38

Hardy first became aware of a salty taste, then in the distance, he heard what he thought was a train horn. Something pressed against his throat and abdomen. He looked to the front and saw trees—all pointing in the wrong direction. He was hanging upside down in his seat belt harness.

He heard moaning, turned his head slowly, and saw Ben suspended in the harness.

"Are you okay?"

"Where are we?" Ben asked haltingly.

"Upside down."

"I can't move my arm."

Hardy flexed his arms, legs and feet. His only pain was in his tongue, which he had bitten. With one hand, he held onto the shoulder harness and with the other unsnapped the seat belt and dropped to the roof. Quickly, but carefully, he freed Ben from his seat belt, gently lowering him.

"You okay, buddy?" Ben moaned In response. Hardy drew back and began kicking at the safety glass windshield. He landed several hard strikes with his heel before it gave way. He dragged Ben through the opening. Ben's left arm dangled like a noodle just below where the humerus protruded against the skin. What had at first sounded like a train whistle, was a car horn in the distance. Hardy reached inside Ben's jacket and slipped his 9 mm from the shoulder holster. He splinted Ben's arm with a stick he found on the ground and secured it with his necktie. Ben kept up a constant moaning and just as he finished binding the limp arm to the makeshift splint, Ben rolled to his side and vomited into the snow.

"Oh, God, Jackson, it hurts like hell," he gasped.

"Common, you're going to make it. Here, let's do you a sling."

Hardy tore the lining from his coat and fashioned a crude sling, then got him to his feet.

"Hold to my belt and let's climb out of here," Hardy said.

Ben grabbed the back of Hardy's waistband with his right hand and they inched their way through the snow up the mountain and onto the road where they hobbled toward the blaring car horn.

The Mercedes had apparently hit an icy spot and lost control. Black skid marks led to where the car had left the road and sailed down the wooded slope. Hardy squinted down into the direction of the horn sound. He saw the Mercedes resting at a 30-degree angle between two spruces, the front end smashed into the trunk of one of the trees. The force of the impact had sprung open all four doors.

"Do you see them?" Ben asked.

"No. Come on, let's get out of here and find a doctor for you."

"Not before I determine if they're dead."

"Are you nuts?" Hardy said. "You could lose that arm."

"This isn't half as bad as the leg wound I received in Vietnam."

"Have we got to do this?"

"Yes."

"Can't we wait for our reinforcements?"

"No. We can't wait."

"Let me check it out."

Hardy crouched low and crept toward the back of the car. He stopped and listened, but could detect no movement. He moved along the left side of the car and peeked in the rear window. The driver was draped over the steering wheel with his bloody face smashed against the shattered windshield. He wasn't moving. Hardy crept closer, looked at Wolfgang who was sitting limp in the seat belt harness, then moved near the driver where he squatted down and observed the brute awhile. Seeing no sign of life, he pressed his finger to the man's jugular vein. Dead. Looking down, he saw the butt of a Luger protruding from beneath a roll of belly fat. He removed it, pulled the dead man back off the horn and motioned for Ben.

Ben stumbled forward. "Are they dead?"

"The big one. I don't know about Wolfgang."

They walked around to the passenger side and looked in. Wolfgang's head was hanging limp, chin against his chest. Blood oozed from his mouth. He was either unconscious or dead. Hardy poked Wolfgang's head with the barrel of the Luger. "Hey, asshole."

Wolfgang's lips moved and he moaned.

"He's alive!" Ben said.

"Unfortunately." Hardy lifted Wolfgang's right arm and felt his pulse. It was weak. "Probably in shock. He may have internal injuries." He examined him further, starting at his head and moving downward. "His leg looks like it's broken just below the knee. Looks pretty bad. Jesus Christ! What do we do?"

"Nothing." Ben said.

"Leave him?"

"Why not?"

Wolfgang moaned. "Help me," he whispered.

Hardy looked at Ben who was cradling his broken arm. Ben turned away, avoiding his gaze and looked up the mountain toward the road. Twilight was falling. "I haven't heard a car go by since we wrecked," Ben said. "If we don't get out of here quickly, we'll have to spend the night. And it gets cold in these mountains."

"Well, yeah, but what do we do with this piece of shit?" Hardy said jerking his thumb toward Wolfgang.

"I say we leave him." Ben said. "You and I can walk out of here before night, but not with him."

"Here," Hardy handed the Luger to Ben. "Shoot him."

* * * *

At a small airport outside Berchtesgaden, Hermann Blucker and the Raven Group waited inside a hangar for Wolfgang to arrive. The plan was to fly to a small landing strip outside Munich then motor to the city. Blucker paced, his head bowed. His cane tapped out a rhythm on the concrete floor. He stopped abruptly and looked at his watch for what seemed like the hundredth time and then glanced out the window with a shudder of revulsion at Frederick.

The American, pacing outside, spat out a soggy wad of tobacco, where it steamed on new-fallen show like a fresh deposit of dog shit.

"I do not like this. Wolfgang should have been here."

"Are you certain that he received the message to meet us here?" Willy Gleck asked.

"I talked to him myself," snapped Blucker.

"It could be only one thing," said Klaus Kluge. "The Americans. Somehow they have learned of our plans and kidnapped Wolfgang or…"

Blucker turned to Klaus. "What time did Frau Schradmann say they departed Kitzbuhel?"

"2:15. Shall I inquire again to see if she's heard from them?"

"*Ja.* Do that. Also call all police and ask if there have been any automobile accidents between here and Kitzbuhel."

* * * *

Ben stared at the Luger in Hardy's outstretched hand for a long time, then turned toward Wolfgang. "Help me get the bastard out of the car."

Hardy crammed the pistol behind his belt and went to the car, unsnapped the seat belt and pulled Wolfgang out and stretched him out on the ground. He had lost a lot of blood and was barely conscious.

Hardy and Ben sat down on a nearby rock ledge where the snow had melted off and stared at Wolfgang. "Now what do we do?" asked Hardy.

"We came here to stop them. Let's kill him now." He itched to blow the bastard's brains out.

Ben grimaced with pain. "We don't know why he was going to Eagle's Nest. Maybe it was to meet someone. There may be someone searching for him this very minute. We may have to use him for a bargaining chip. It's not like we got much to fight with. I'm totally worthless with my arm like this."

Hardy's eyes bore into the dusky forest's gloom in all directions but could detect no one. He looked back at Wolfgang on the ground. "He'll freeze tonight if we leave him uncovered."

"God's will be done. He's already a dead man."

"What do you mean?"

"Our government will never permit him to return to Munich," Ben said. "We can save the CIA a lot of time and trouble by letting him die right here and take our chances making our way to safety through the cover of trees out of sight of the roadway."

They had just begun to make their way down the icy road when Hardy cocked his head.

"Listen. I hear something!"

"What?"

Hardy turned his ear toward the approaching sound. "A car—it's a car!" A long, silver-gray Mercedes with tinted windows rounded the curve from the direction of Eagle's Nest. Hardy grabbed Ben and they dove for cover.

The Mercedes stopped several yards up the road. The back door opened and a tall man stepped out and he heard muffled voices of alarm as the occupants spied the wreckage and the semi-conscious Wolfgang on the ground.

Hardy froze in his tracks. The voice was chillingly familiar.

The front passenger door opened and a younger man climbed out, turned and assisted an elderly man in glasses and with a cane from the car seat. The older one made his way to Wolfgang.

"Heil, Hitler!"

"Help me."

All eyes turned to the struggling Wolfgang. "Get them. Get them," he muttered feebly. "They ran that way."

"They're coming!" Hardy whispered to Ben. "Can you get up and move?"

"No, I'll never make it," croaked Ben. "You go. Now! Only you have a chance."

Hardy dragged Ben behind a fallen tree and lit out with the sound of running feet close behind.

Shots rang out and Hardy turned to see a winded Klaus nearly on him. Hardy, crouching low, barreled headlong into Klaus. The Luger from the back of his belt slipped out and cracked onto the pavement at Klaus's feet. Hardy made a grab for the gun and a heavy-buckled boot came down on his hand, nearly crushing the bones against the asphalt.

"Christ! My hand!" cried Hardy.

Hardy jerked backward, pulling his hand free, but scraping most of the skin off, as the now familiar younger man laughed and grabbed for his throat and slipped the 9 mm from the front of Hardy's belt. Hardy socked out with his fist at the man's midsection and caught him soundly in the groin.

"You miserable fucker!" the man screamed.

Hardy knew where he had encountered him before. That night in the semi-darkness of the cotton gin. He knew the oaf to be strong as an ox, but just as clumsy. While the man remained doubled grabbing at his crotch, Hardy swept his foot around in back of his heels and pushed him back by the shoulders, knocking him to the pavement.

The others were too busy in their concern for Wolfgang to heed the struggle or notice when he fled. As he scrambled off the side of the road, down an embankment and into the trees, he searched frantically for Ben, who was nowhere in sight. He heard excited German voices and the report of a Luger just as bark exploded off a nearby tree. And then another shot rang out. He heard car doors slam and the fading sound of the Mercedes as it sped away.

* * * *

"Jackson...Jackson."

The words were barely audible. He looked to his right, to where he heard his name and saw Ben lying crumpled on his right side. He scrambled over to him.

"Ben, are you alright?"

"I can't move," he groaned.

"What's wrong? Are you hit?"

"I can't move."

Hardy ran his hand under Ben's shoulders to straighten him and felt a warm stickiness. He looked down and beneath Ben's shoulders saw a large spot of bright red staining the snow.

"Where are you hit?"

"Between my shoulders."

"We need to get you out of here. Can you get up?"

"I can't move my legs. The bullet must have cut my spinal cord."

"What about your arms?"

"I'm paralyzed."

"I've got to get you out of here." He ran his arms beneath Ben and scooped him up, staggered a few steps, stumbled and fell.

"Both of us will never make it," Ben whispered. "Leave me and go."

"I can't do that."

"There is no need for both of us to die."

He was right, but Hardy said nothing. He picked Ben up and stumbled forward a few more yards and fell again. He heard voices. He snapped his head around and cocked an ear. The voices were growing louder. The Germans were back.

"You must escape," Ben whispered haltingly. "Someone must live to tell."

"I can't leave you."

"I can't make it out of here...you can. It's important that you live."

Hardy looked into Ben's pleading eyes.

"I have only one request."

"What?" Hardy asked hoarsely.

"Don't let...*them*...kill me."

"I can't do that!"

"I would do it for you. Please."

"Shut the fuck up!" Hardy growled.

"They're coming," Ben said. "Do it now!"

Hardy heard them also.

"Please hurry," Ben begged. "Hardy, God, I'm dead already. If the Germans don't kill me, I'll bleed to death."

He eased Ben to the ground and looked at his bloodstained hands. They were thick and strong and could kill a man with the right kind of blow. But he couldn't.

"Jackson! Now!"

Hardy searched frantically until he spied a brown rock the size of a shoe box. He brought it to where his new friend lay.

"*Semper Fi.*"

"*Semper Fi,*" said Hardy.

Chapter 39

Hardy stumbled on through the tall pines, the morning light barely trickling through the dense, black trunks to show the way. But he dare not take to the road again. He knew from the map that there was a tourist rest area part way up the mountain on the way to the Eagle's Nest. He didn't know if it were manned this time of year, but if no one was there, he might follow the tree line up behind it and break in and take shelter until he figured out his next move.

Christ, his feet were so cold he couldn't feel them anymore. He wiggled—or thought he wiggled—his toes inside the ankle-high, lace-up boots. He tried not to think back to his last sight of Ben. He pushed the ghastly image to the back of his mind. Eventually, he'd have to deal with it, but not now. Ben was right. One of them had to make it out alive.

The morning wore on and the dim amber light grew to a yellow-white brilliance and no longer slanted through the pines, but seemed to be coming from directly overhead. He saw patches of color ahead. Green and red.

Hardy wove through the dense forest that grew almost to the back door of a brightly painted building. There was no activity that he could see. The back of the building was all brick with a metal door and a large trash container outside. He dared not go to the front of the building where the two-lane Kehlstein Road wound past on its way to the top of the mountain and the Eagle's Nest. Wolfgang and his band of merrymakers just might be headed past and he didn't need to run into them. He would be no match for them and he doubted he had the strength to outrun them.

Hardy listened for awhile, but all he heard was the ghostly whisper of wind through the tops of the towering pines and ancient cedars that enclosed the slight clearing in back of the building on three sides. He crept toward the metal door of the brick building and gave it a tug, but it was locked tight. Off to his right was a small metal storage shed. He approached it to find a flimsy padlock securing the door.

Hardy ventured back into the forest and found a sturdy hardwood branch. He wedged the branch under the hasp and pried. The lock was stronger than it appeared. At last, the hasp popped with a loud snap and the door swung free.

Hardy stooped slightly to duck into the low door and paused for a moment to let his eyes adjust to the inner gloom. An unlocked wooden chest stood in one corner. He flipped back the lid and pawed through miscellaneous hammers and shrub clippers until his hand closed around the cold steel of a crowbar. At least he would go down swinging its wicked hooked claw, if he couldn't use it for anything else. He carried the crowbar to the brick building and wedged the tip of the crowbar into the narrow space between the door and door jam. If he were able to pry the door he might set off a burglar alarm that would bring the authorities, or there might be a phone inside to call for help. He had to get in.

Hardy pushed on the end of the crowbar until sweat popped out on his forehead and the hair on the back of his head grew wet and stuck to his neck. Still he pushed. At last, the door sprang free. He rushed inside a backroom stacked high with cartons and banged the door closed behind him, but the sprung lock wouldn't latch and the door swung back open. He slid a carton over to hold the door shut and went exploring.

A few seconds passed, then a distant, faint beeping erupted into a screeching wail as the burglar alarm went off. Only a few minutes now.

The door from the storeroom led to an area behind the counter. Noonday sun streamed through plate glass windows.

Suddenly, Hardy was ravenous. He grabbed some chocolate bars off a rack near the counter and clawed at the wrappers, woofing down three before he stopped long enough to taste the waxy-sweet chocolate. He ran his tongue over the roof of his mouth and jerked open a cooler, grabbed a bottled water and gulped down half.

"Jesus! That's good," he breathed, wiping his arm across his mouth and beginning to rummage for something else to eat.

The deafening alarm continued to scream on and he held his fingers in his ears. He didn't know how much more he could take of the penetrating siren that seemed to pound a spike of sound deep into his throbbing brain. He'd wait outside. As he dashed for the back door, he caught sight through the window of a silver Mercedes pulling up. The driver's door swung open and Kluge climbed out.

Hardy thought his heart stopped.

Kluge turned toward the shrill sound coming from the building and shaded his one good eye with his hand, craning to see inside. He motioned to someone inside the car, and the unkempt American he encountered before climbed out the other side.

They both drew guns and began to walk toward the back of the building. Hardy remembered the unlocked back door and knew he had to get out fast. He looked around frantically for something to use as a battering ram and spied a heavy metal stool behind the counter. He snatched up the stool and ran headlong toward the plate glass front door. He connected with a solid "crack!" and a spider-web pattern of cracks fanned out from the point of impact, but the glass didn't give way. He heard the faint rumble of falling cartons beneath the piercing shriek of the alarm.

"Damn! I'm going to die like a cornered rat." Hardy had lost so much in the last year, but shit, it couldn't end like this.

With a ragged growl, Hardy ran with the heavy stool once more against the cracked glass and the glass gave way. He leapt forward and kicked remaining shards out as he burst through. In the open air, he bolted for the trees on the other side of the road and heard the bark of guns and felt bullets whizzing by him. He dove for the ditch and rolled, scrambling up the other side and into a thick pine growth.

"Hey, shit-for-brains!" called the panting American as he pursued Hardy into the woods. "We gotcha now. You got something that belongs to us. We're gonna kill your scrawny lawyer ass, but first you're going to give it up."

On he plunged into the darkening forest and knew that if he didn't keep some point of reference he could be lost forever as the dense woods closed behind him. Hardy ran toward where there was more light off to his right and spied through the trunks a road running along the edge of the woods. Keeping the road in sight, he swerved through the trees.

God, his lungs were bursting and bile bubbled up into his throat, filling his mouth with sourness, but he could hear the heavy breaking of brush and branches behind him. He chanced a glance backward, and couldn't see the source of the noise. But he knew they were close behind.

"Hey, you! Fuck face!" a hoarse voice echoed through the trees. "Betcha can't see me, but we're gaining on your cute redneck ass. Give it up now and die easy or keep playing your game. Don't make no difference to me. I like to play games. And I can teach ya some we played in the pen."

Hardy heard a car on the road to his right and saw the Mercedes creeping along even with him. He continued to dip and sway around trunks. He felt something catch at his ankle, winding like a rope around his boot and he pitched forward, scraping his cheek on rough tree bark on his way down. Christ! He thrashed on the forest floor, his feet entangled in a web of vines.

He grew light-headed with the struggle to free himself like one caught in a nightmarish run to escape an unseen monster on legs gone to jelly. Hardy clawed at the vines to free his feet. He struggled to his feet and heard a loud crashing of brush nearby.

He leapt forward and looked quickly back to see the sweating, shirt-sleeved American not ten yards behind. The loud report of a gun echoed in the semidarkness and bark splintered from a tree overhead and rained down particles. He plunged on, and two more shots ricocheted and missed. But the American was gaining on him. There appeared to be a clearing ahead.

Hardy stumbled out into the clearing, but knew he had to find cover fast because he was an easy target out in the open. He'd had good legs once on the playing field, but that was twenty years ago. If he were to be a target, then he'd be a moving target. He bolted in a zigzagging pattern across the rolling field, hoping to make it to one of the few buildings that dotted the landscape.

The terrain and buildings began to look familiar and he knew he'd seen photos of this area before. He had stumbled on to the former Obersalzberg, the compound for Hitler and his top officers and henchmen. Shots rang out behind him and he dove across a knoll and rolled into some shrubbery, where he scrambled on hands and knees deeper into the brush. Briars ripped at his palms and shredded the knees of his corduroy pants.

He could hear the pounding of feet on sod and knew he had to move soon or die right here. He peered through the brush and saw the back of what appeared to be a large, cream stucco chalet with diagonally striped shutters and a cedar shake roof about a hundred yards ahead. A van with Hotel Zum Turken stenciled on the side was parked near a service entrance. If it were some sort of public building, it was bound to be open. Maybe the driver had left the keys in the truck ignition.

Hardy could hear the American panting so near. He had stopped for a breath and looked as though he was getting his bearings.

"Hey, Mr. Redneck hick lawyer! You're dead, ya know?"

He could make out the shape of his pursuer through the brush. The one they called Frederick glanced one way then another, trying to figure out which bush harbored his prey.

Hardy lucked out when the lumbering ox took off at a trot in an opposite direction. He broke from his cover and ran faster than he could ever remember running in his life toward the chalet. His chest hurt, and the jarring of his piston-pounding legs felt like it would drive his brains through the top of his skull. Only a few more yards now.

Shots rang out and the bullet pinged the metal of the truck panel. Hardy ducked behind the van then peered in the driver's window to see if the keys were in the ignition. No keys. Shit!

He scrambled toward the back door and gave a tremendous tug on the large wrought iron pull, but the door held fast. Hardy spied a button by the door and pressed it frantically.

"Come on, come on!," and he pounded his fists against the thick timber door. The door suddenly swung open and a portly woman in a white apron scowled in exasperation.

"Vat is it?"

He pushed by the startled woman, who stumbled backward, and he fled by huge stainless steel refrigerators and into a warm, fragrant kitchen, where a tall man grabbed for him. He shoved the man aside into a work island hung with clanking copper pots and kept on his way.

"Call for help!?" Hardy commanded, but the surprised kitchen help stared dumbly after him. He swung back toward the slender man and seized the lapels of his black vest and screamed in his face once more, "Call for help! Do you understand?"

Hardy released the breathless man just as a violent pounding began against the back door. He sprinted into a lobby area where stained glass window lights framing a massive front door cast their jewel tones upon a thick carpet already resplendent with swirling patterns of golden vines and stags.

The mellow glow of a chandelier lit the pale yellow walls of an adjoining hallway and Hardy fled toward the inviting passage. On his left, elaborate sliding brass screens shielded elevator doors. To his right, was a long hallway with a solid-looking door at the end, stenciled with "Verboten". Hardy ran headlong for the door, throwing his shoulder against it while he turned the latch.

The door swung open into semi-darkness.

He heard someone call, "Stop! Stop!" and he slammed the door shut behind him and threw the bolt. As his eyes adjusted to the dim light, he saw highly polished tile floors and amber-shaded wall sconces glowing against pale stucco walls that rounded into a smooth, vaulted ceiling. On the far end of the landing an ornate iron railing rimmed a downward flight of stairs.

Hardy leaped toward the stairs, grabbed the railing and pivoted down three steps. Loud pounding came from the door and he knew if enough weight were applied, the bolt would splinter the wood. He descended stone steps rapidly as the air around him grew ever more dank and cold. He shivered in the cave-like stillness of what seemed an endless maze of high-ceilinged passageways. Every few yards a bare light bulb hung from ceiling conduit, casting an eerie glow, lighting his way through a gloom that led he knew not where. Heavy-hung doors to rooms led off this way and that and sharp turns in corridors held recessed caverns like miniature gun turrets.

He realized that he had stumbled into what could only be the remnants of Hitler's elaborate bunker system. He knew much had been destroyed by the advancing Allies and by the German people themselves years after the war in an attempt to erase this evil blight from the countryside, if not from the historical record. What was left intact was amazingly preserved.

Rapid footsteps echoed behind him and he fled on, going deeper and deeper into the recesses of this subterranean network of manmade mole runs. He rounded a corner and ran smack into a door that wouldn't budge. There was nowhere to backtrack or corridors leading off in other directions. There was nothing. He had no weapon.

He glanced around for anything he could use to fend off the coming attack and spied a wooden crate in the corner. It wasn't much, but crap, what else did he have?

Hardy pushed the crate under the bare light bulb at the end of the hallway and unscrewed the bulb. He gave a jerk on the cord, hoping to pop off enough to fashion a garrote. He pulled out a length of the tough cord from metal conduit, but it didn't break. Echoing footfalls and voices reached him and he knew his pursuers had to be just one corridor bend behind. He stomped the crate into kindling and came up with a slat, rusty nails curling like a claw from the end.

Just then, Frederick burst around the last bend and he could see his silhouetted bull-like form charging in for the kill and firing his weapon with wild abandon, shots ricocheting off walls, ceilings, floor. Now was no time for wasted motion. He ducked bullets and waited his chance. When the American was nearly on him, Hardy sprang up and swung the crate slat backhand across the side of his attacker's face. The rusty nail raked his flesh, catching the corner of his eye and tearing diagonally across his cheek.

"You miserable little mother-fucker!" Frederick dropped his gun, screamed and grabbed at his face as blood poured through his fingers. With a roar, the American came at him again, grabbing the wrist that held the shattered slat, squeezing and twisting, while the other hand clamped Hardy's throat in a vice-like grip.

The pain was horrible. He was no match for the superior strength of the enraged skinhead. Hardy kicked out, aiming for the man's groin, but couldn't get enough leverage to find his mark. Next, he kicked with his heel on the man's kneecap, and this time he hit home and heard the leg pop with the sudden, violent backward bowing.

His attacker released his grip on Hardy's throat and bent double, vomiting on the stone floor. Hardy sprang forward, grabbed each ear and slammed the creep's head back into the wall. As he thrashed about semiconscious, Hardy searched for the dropped gun. Just then, a sharp blow struck Hardy in the back of the knee, and when he tried to regain his footing, he slid in the American's slimy puke and crashed against a wall.

Frederick lumbered up on his one good leg while supporting himself against the wall. Hardy rolled away quickly and came up on his feet. He'd have to make sure this fat, Neo-Nazi bastard went down and didn't get back up.

The electrical cord and socket dangled before his eyes, and Hardy gave it another jerk, but it wouldn't come free. He sprang toward the weakened man, slamming a fist hard against his temple.

The American hit the floor like a sack of shit. Hardy couldn't believe his pursuers hadn't called for backups. And they probably threatened or killed that simpleton and the cook in the hotel so they hadn't called for help.

Frederick moaned on the floor as he came awake. Hardy bent and took hold of him under the armpits, hoisting him to his feet. *Christ! The asshole weighs a ton!*

He'd never be able to support his weight with one hand and wrap the cord around his neck with the other. Hardy staggered backward with the dead weight in his arms. He slid one hand around his chest and grabbed for one of the man's loosely dangling hands, feeling for his fleshy index finger.

Hardy raised the limp finger toward the open socket, and after a couple of feeble stabs, poked it firmly into the outlet. As the current passed through Frederick, his body jerked and stiffened, but the juice hit Hardy, too, because he couldn't release fast enough.

The pair went straight down with a crash. Hardy lay there dazed, but alive under Frederick's limp body. He crawled out to the acrid stench of cooked flesh. He didn't know if he had finished him off, but he wouldn't be getting up any time soon.

Hardy patted the dark floor until his hand closed over the cold metal of a gun handle. He raised the SIG Sauer up and examined it appreciatively.

"Good taste in guns," said Hardy, kicking Frederick's out-flung arm out of the way. "Lucky for me you couldn't shoot for shit."

Hardy turned and began to leave the end of the bunker, but turned back and rifled through the American's pockets for another ammunition clip. Finding what he was looking for, he snapped in the fresh clip and headed out.

At the top of the stairs, the door hung ajar from the splintered door jam, allowing the warm, yellow light to spill through into the cold landing. He peeked cautiously out, and seeing no one, ventured into the hallway. He stopped under the archway leading to the lobby and spied the angular form of the hotel employee he had earlier asked for help lying sprawled face up on the dark green carpet on the other side of an ornately carved walnut table. A dark stain spread out from his head, turning one of the carpet's golden stags crimson. A large vase lay shattered nearby.

All was deathly quiet. Hardy clutched the gun to his chest and moved stealthily along the wall toward the kitchen and the odor of scorched food. He crept toward the back door and saw nothing but the abandoned van.

He turned and made his way back to the lobby, stepping over the dead hotel man and toward the front door. He pressed flat against the wall as he peered through the stained-glass sidelights. He saw Klaus Kluge pacing nervously, smoking and with a cell phone to his ear. The Mercedes sat in the circular drive and a figure, which must have been Wolfgang, had his head flung back against the seat, occasionally rolling it from side to side.

Shit! Weren't there any cops in this whole damn country? Didn't the alarm in the tourist stop bring someone? And what about that welcoming party of good guys that was supposed to be awaiting them just outside Munich? Why didn't this group of erstwhile citizens call for an ambulance to take their precious leader for help with his busted leg? Nothing had made sense since he stumbled on the worthless reichsmarks in Jabo's attic. How could a bunch of pukes like this think they could regain a hold on the world after the horror of 50 years ago?

Hardy went back to the kitchen and slid out the back door. He pressed his back flat against the rough stucco and slid along the house under cover of thick shrubbery until he worked himself to the front of the hotel. He caught the tone of Kluge's voice as he barked angrily into the cell phone. His hand clutching the big gun shook so violently, he was afraid he couldn't pick the pacing German off from this distance.

Kluge turned in his pacing and scowled back toward the hotel. The old man was pale and he seemed to move with great difficulty. He folded the cell phone and angrily jammed it in an inside coat pocket, turned and jerked toward the front door.

Hardy heard the heavy door click shut behind him and he ventured cautiously out into the open, walking straight for the Mercedes. The car's back door swung slowly open as he approached, and one finely-shod foot eased out onto the drive. Wolfgang rose sneering out of the backseat, shakily supported by the car door, and brought his gun up, steadying it on the top of the doorframe. He was taking unsteady aim, when Hardy stopped, brought the SIG Sauer up in both hands.

"Stop! Stop!," screamed a feeble old man struggling out the other side of the car. Hardy jumped at the sound of his cry, but resolutely squeezed off a shot.

The bullet split Wolfgang's forehead from ten yards away, as brain matter, blood and bone exploded across the hood of the car. Hardy swung toward the old man, but didn't fire. The one they had called Blucker hobbled around the back of the car, coming upon the prostrate form of Wolfgang.

Blucker dropped down on one knee and then the other. Seemingly oblivious to Hardy, he gathered Wolfgang's ruined head in his hands, muttering and crooning unintelligibly. He swayed, laid the shattered skull of the would-be Fuhrer tenderly upon the gravel drive. He struggled to his feet, his bloody claw-like hands sliding on the car door as he grabbed at it for support. He stared glassily at Hardy and then at the forgotten Glock lying by Wolfgang's body at his feet. The old man crouched and retrieved the gun.

Hardy stood watching the slow-motion tableau, and as Blucker shakily raised the Glock toward him, he also raised his gun. But Blucker appeared to have used up his strength, and his hand dropped limply to the side of his withered thigh. His face a sickly gray, beads of sweat popped out on his forehead and upper lip. He suddenly clutched at the front of his coat and seemed to curl like melting wax as he slid gasping to the ground beside Wolfgang's body.

"You!" screamed Kluge from behind Hardy and he swung around, gun blazing. However, Kluge had gotten off the first shot and Hardy didn't know where his own shot went because of a tremendous piercing pain in his shoulder that flung him back against the front fender of the Mercedes.

Hardy struggled to right himself and rolled off the fender onto the ground on his hands and knees, scrambling for his gun in the gravel. His hand closed over the gun handle and he braced for the next shot, but when he looked up he saw Kluge crumpled on the front lawn, not fifteen feet away.

Hardy made his way to Kluge, blood coursing down his left arm from where the bullet had torn through. He knelt staring down at what was left of Kluge's face and knew the last of the old Germans was gone.

Chapter 40

Hardy shifted uncomfortably in the cramped airline seat, trying to find a comfortable position for his shoulder and arm. It still hurt like hell, but he was going home. Outside the window, the Atlantic stretched across the horizon. He rested his head on the back of the seat and closed his eyes. God, he never remembered being this exhausted.

He kept remembering Ben's pleading eyes. When he thought of what came after, there was only an empty numbness.

Now he was going home.

Someone nudged his shoulder. He cracked an eye and looked around. It was the guy with the flattop in the gray suit. "Mr. Jackson, we'll be landing at Andrews in one hour. From there, you'll be taken to Washington for debriefing."

Hardy's eyes narrowed, "By whom?"

"I'm not privy to that information, sir."

"I've already been debriefed once, and I'm going home."

"Sir, my instructions are to deliver you to the proper officials at Andrews."

Hardy felt uneasy. "Can't it wait?"

"No, sir."

* * * *

The jet touched down smoothly at Andrews and Hardy stepped out into the marvelous day. The serious guy with the flattop was standing at the backdoor of an idling black limousine.

"Over here, sir."

Hardy stooped and looked inside at a rangy, thin man. On the opposite seat was a tall, big-boned woman in thick glasses. He didn't recognize the man, but he would know the Attorney General anywhere.

The man offered his hand. "Mr. Jackson. I'm Jacob Jaffee, Office of Special Investigations, Department of Justice. I've been looking forward to meeting you. Would you please join us for the ride to Washington?"

"Pardon me if I don't jump right in, but I've recently developed an aversion to getting into cars with strangers."

Jaffee flashed a laminated ID with photo and badge and gestured toward the woman. "This is the Attorney General of the United States."

"Hello, Mr. Jackson," she said offering her hand. "I've heard a lot about you."

Hardy crawled into the backseat next to Jaffee, facing the AG. Jaffee pecked on the glass and the limo rolled forward. Jaffee made small talk at first. When they were on the interstate cruising toward Washington, he turned to Hardy.

"Ben was one of my finest men. His death was a great loss to our office and to me personally. I've read the debriefing report wired from Salzburg. Thank you for your assistance."

"Sure," answered Hardy.

"Have you discussed any of these matters with anyone?" Jaffee's tone had turned brusque.

"Just the people in Salzburg."

Jaffee nodded.

The AG leaned forward and said, "Mr. Jackson, it is a matter of the highest national security that you never speak or write of what you saw, heard or experienced, other than at debriefings by authorized government agents."

It took a second for the full import of her statement to hit.

"Pardon me, ma'am, but you know, First Amendment and all that."

"Mr. Jackson, the information you are privy to is so sensitive to national security that it overrides everything else."

"I'm to forget that Sylvia Birch and Ben were murdered?" He was incredulous.

"It's unfortunate that Mrs. Birch died. But skiing accidents do happen."

"She was brutally murdered."

"Our embassy has done a thorough investigation of the matter," said Jaffee, "And their report will show that Mrs. Birch died as a result of an accident."

"And Ben? What's the official spin on his death?"

"We thought perhaps you could enlighten us on that subject."

Both blankly eyed Hardy. He shifted in the seat. "I've already told the people at the consulate in Salzburg what happened. Like I said, after Ben was shot and paralyzed, I barely escaped."

"It's odd that the Nazis would crush his skull with a stone when they obviously had a pistol," said Jaffee. "Don't you think, Mr. Jackson?"

Hardy said nothing but stared unblinking into Jaffee's eyes.

"The official report will say that Ben was robbed and murdered," Jaffee said.

"No one would believe such a story," replied Hardy.

Jaffee and the AG said nothing.

"Now I see. If I don't cooperate I get pinned with Ben's murder?"

"Now, Mr. Jackson. We aren't interested in causing you trouble. We do wish you to remain silent," said Jaffee. "And, of course, there's that bit of unfinished business in Huntsville surrounding the Doolittle murder investigation, your fingerprints in his room, and all. At last count, there were…how many? About five deaths in which you are directly implicated? The bodies are piling up, Mr. Jackson. It could become complicated for you if someone starts digging to the bottom of the pile."

"And what if I decide not to go along with your story?"

"I think that would be most unwise, Mr. Jackson. After all, the Neo-Nazi movement is still very active in some parts of the world."

The AG quietly added, "The Justice Department is prepared to offer you a new identity and relocation under the witness protection program and a liberal stipend for two years."

"What about the document?" Hardy asked.

"Of course," said the AG. "Our government will quietly access the funds in the Swiss account and see that it is placed in a Jewish reparations fund."

Hardy sat silently for a long time, looking out the window at the passing green countryside.

"Can we count on you, Mr. Jackson?" she asked.

Chapter 41

Northern New Mexico. December 4, 1996.

His breath comes in fast, sharp puffs and his arms ache with the weight of the rock above his head. And he struggles to bring it down upon the gray-flecked head below, struggling against unseen forces with the last of his waning strength. But he propels his watery muscles to do as they are bidden and the ruby flesh of the ripe watermelon explodes onto the immaculate snow. Boyhood friends laugh and scoop great bloody handfuls to their mouths as he screams for them to stop.

"Hardy! Hardy! For Christ's sake, baby, stop fighting me. Wake up, darling! Wake up!"

Sarah is holding him immobile against her. "Hardy Jackson, when will you ever tell someone about this nightmare?"

He says nothing as his breathing slows and he forces the trembling to stop as he inhales her sweet scent in the darkness. Yet again he must unravel the events of the past year. So much seems unreal. Could it have been just a year? Yes, just a year. He twisted to look at the glowing red numbers on the nightstand—nearly 5 a.m. Might as well get up.

* * * *

One week later Hardy slouched low at mid-morning in a worn, brown stuffed chair, his tan antelope boots propped on the coffee table, lost in his thoughts and writing on a yellow legal pad. Juniper wood sputtered and burned slowly in the kiva fireplace, filling the room with its warm sweetness. A hot coal popped onto the red tile floor. He glanced up, saw that it was no danger, yawned and stretched. He looked out the west window, over the tops of ponderosa pines and quaken aspen, across the wide expanse below where the Rio Grande River had carved its path in the desert floor eons ago. It had begun to snow, flakes big as nickels drifting straight down. He checked his watch. Already 11 a.m. He'd been writing for over three hours. When the writing was going well, time flew. He laid his pen and pad aside and watched the snow fill the branches of the pines.

Sarah would be home later. She had been down in Santa Fe since Monday attending a refresher course, getting ready to take the New Mexico bar exam. She already had a job lined up with the Taos County Public Defenders Office.

They were married in Las Vegas six months ago today. The feds had relocated them north of Taos, given them a new identity—Jackson Lee was his new name—a liberal monthly stipend and a nice adobe style home on the western slope of the Sangre de Cristo. Sarah liked the climate and the laid-back lifestyle. The only new item she had added to her wardrobe was sandals, which she wore with white socks.

Jasmine was in preschool and happy. The marriage had required big adjustments and the relationship was bumpy. Sarah had been on her own for quite awhile. She needed what she calls her "down time" when she goes off into some place inside herself where there's no room for anyone else. But when she comes back, it's worth the wait. She returns from her emotional sabbaticals with the exuberance of a child and the greedy hunger of a starving waif.

He'd come to expect different things from a woman, from a relationship. He still cherished Millie's memory. In their 21 years together, Millie had become like a favorite sweater, warm and embracing comfort at the end of a cold day. He missed that in Sarah.

Sarah was like a new pair of shoes. They feel so good in the store, but after awhile they begin to pinch and rub. Sarah challenged him, and sometimes he came away from their sparring feeling a little battered. But she was made of good stuff and if he had to reshape his expectations, he knew in time the two of them would fit as closely in the day as they did in the night.

Fit as closely as when she clasped him to stop the trembling when once again he brought the rock down.

0-595-31370-1

Printed in the United States
27718LVS00003B/177